Mary Mackie was born and educated in Lincoln, and after living in West Germany, North Yorkshire, North Devon, North Wales, and Lincolnshire again, she now resides in Norfolk. She is married to Chris with two sons and two grandchildren.

Since first being published in 1971, Mary Mackie has produced nearly seventy books for various publishers in the UK and the USA. Her work has been translated into over twenty languages and has appeared in large print, on audio cassette and in serialisations. Her novel *The Clouded Land* was shortlisted for the RNA Award in 1995. She has also written two best-selling non-fiction titles.

Mary enjoys being a new grandmother, the Norfolk countryside, local history, meeting people, scribbling in coffee shops, reading, irreverent comedy and strong well-plotted drama. She also dabbles in poetry for fun. Mary says she hates housework and gardening, ungrammatical and impenetrable prose, and undisciplined children(!).

SWEETER THAN WINE

Katarin was spellbound. He was here, in the flesh; the Baron von Drachensberg was tall, compelling and definitely interested in her. When she'd returned to the land of her ancestors to run a family vineyard, Katarin never expected to be so drawn to this renowned womaniser. When he was elected Wine King to her Queen for the local festival, Katarin found herself constantly in his magnetic presence. Could she spark his love and control her desire before the King and Queen participated in the final ceremony — an ancient celebration rumoured to end in pagan fertility rites?

MARY MACKIE

SWEETER THAN WINE

Complete and Unabridged

ULVERSCROFT
Leicester

First published in Great Britain in 1997 by
Severn House Publishers Limited
Surrey

First Large Print Edition
published 1998
by arrangement with
Severn House Publishers Limited
Surrey

British Library CIP Data

Mackie, Mary,
    Sweeter than wine.—Large print ed.—
Ulverscroft large print series: romance
1. Love stories
2. Large type books
I. Title II. Christopher, Mary. Harvest of desire
823.9′14 [F]

ISBN 0–7089–3990–2

Published by
F. A. Thorpe (Publishing) Ltd.
Anstey, Leicestershire
Set by Words & Graphics Ltd.
Anstey, Leicestershire
Printed and bound in Great Britain by
T. J. International Ltd., Padstow, Cornwall

This book is printed on acid-free paper

1

'It's beautiful!' Carol sighed as the trap turned along the river road.

'I thought you'd like it,' Katarin replied somewhat smugly, flicking the reins to remind the pony to keep going. She loved riding out in the brightly painted conveyance, even though it made some of the local people regard her as a typically eccentric *Englischer*.

An occasional car eased past, its occupants sparing a smile for the two young women riding so sedately. Sunlight flashed between the poplars along the river and willows bent over reeds that trembled with the surge of the water. Scarcely a breeze disturbed the warm morning air as the valley drowsed in the sun, rich meadows spreading below terraced slopes where grew row upon row of regimented vines. And on either side dark conifer forests crowned the higher hilltops.

'I still think you're mad to want to settle here,' Carol said. 'Tucked away in the mountains ... It's like stepping back in time. What are you going to do now that you've finished your studies?'

'Help my grandfather run the vineyard, of course,' Katarin replied, smiling beneath the shade of her ribboned straw hat. 'Why else do you think I took all those exams? Viniculture is a very skilled occupation, you know. It will keep me busy.'

'Well, if you say so,' her friend said doubtfully.

'I do say so. It may seem quiet at the moment, but wait until the harvest begins. And there's the wine festival. It's a pity you came in August. You'll miss all the fun.'

'Getting permanently drunk for a week?' Carol inquired with a grin.

'Oh, there's more to it than that. We're steeped in tradition here in Gundelheim. There'll be dancing, music, feasting . . . And you should see the place in wintertime, all the dark trees laden with white. We go skiing, and have ice parties. Bonfires, lanterns, sledges. Even old Blitzen can pull a small sleigh.'

Casting a dubious glance at the plodding pony, Carol said, 'Doesn't 'Blitzen' mean 'lightning'?'

'It does,' Katarin agreed with a smile. 'My grandfather named him. *Opa* has a rather basic sense of humor, I'm afraid . . . And after winter will come spring, with all the valley drowning in blossom — '

2

'All right, all right, you've made your point. But what else is there, apart from work and these merry rural pursuits?'

'What else should I want?' Katarin demanded. 'Oh, look! Kingfisher. See him?'

But the bright blue flash had disappeared among the willows.

Clucking encouragement to the pony, Katarin drove on, a little disturbed to have heard her friend put into words the niggling doubts that she herself had discounted. There did seem to be something missing from her life. Was it David she wanted, or was it something else?

She had left David in England three years before when, after a great deal of heart-searching, she broke her ties with her father's homeland and moved to Germany, to live with her grandfather here on the edge of the Black Forest. Many holidays in Gundelheim had taught her to love the rambling old house and the cool cellars where wine was produced from grapes grown on her grandfather's vineyard, the Maierstufe; so taking a course in vine cultivation and wine-making had seemed a logical step. Now she had passed the course, she was twenty-four years old, and Gundelheim had become her home.

As the trap reached a spot where the

bend of the river lay spread out before
them, with the town on the slope above,
Carol begged her to stop so that she could
take photographs. From that viewpoint the
rooftops and spires of Gundelheim lifted
beyond the orchards that surrounded the
town, with vines parading as a backdrop
and the skyline dark with fir and larch.
On a dark crag commanding the valley, its
turrets and gables etched against a blue sky,
stood Dragon Castle.

'That place looks like something out of a
fairy tale,' Carol remarked.

'Burg Drachen? Yes, it is rather picturesque,
isn't it?'

Carol ruffled a hand through her fair curls.
'Is it open to the public?'

'No, it's a private residence. They say
it used to be the fortress of a robber
baron, back in the Middle Ages. You
can imagine — swordsmen terrorizing the
peasants, demanding taxes and tithes, ravishing
helpless maidens . . .'

'I don't suppose they're still into that sort
of thing, are they?' Carol asked hopefully.
'I wouldn't mind being carried off by some
wicked baron. It would give me something
to tell the girls at the office.'

Katarin laughed. 'Sorry I can't help. The
present family von Drachensberg make their

money from heavy industry. Though some people around here think their blood is still tainted.'

'And is it?'

'No one knows for sure. The old baron wasn't above a bit of underhand dealing, so they say, but he died a couple of months ago. His son has been working in America, so he's a bit of an unknown quantity.'

'They don't sound very dangerous to me,' Carol said. 'I still can't help wondering how you'll stick this out, Katie. I admit it's a lovely area and it all sounds very bucolic, but you used to enjoy a social life and I don't suppose there's much of that out here in the middle of nowhere.'

A car roared up behind the trap, tooting its horn so that Blitzen twitched and increased his pace a fraction. As Katarin glanced round, indicating that the vehicle could pass, the car moved over and the driver blew her a kiss, waving over his shoulder as he drew away, leaving a haze of dust in his wake.

'Someone you know?' Carol asked.

'Bernhard Langren,' Katarin said, tucking a stray strand of copper-gold hair behind her ear before pulling her hat brim lower.

'Oh, yes?' Narrowing her eyes, Carol stared after the departing vehicle. 'Single, is he?'

'So far.'

'Not bad-looking, either, if you like the Nordic type. Do you know him well?'

'Fairly well,' Katarin said with a shrug. 'And you can take that look off your face, Carol Masters. I have enough trouble with Frau Grainau.'

'Who's she?'

'Our daily help. You'll meet her at lunchtime. She thinks Berd and I are ideally suited, just because his family owns a vineyard, too. She sees the time when he will become quite a force in the Wine-Growers' Association, as master of our joint properties, but then Frau Grainau thinks a woman should be interested only in what a man has to offer in the way of worldly goods. Berd's all right, but he doesn't exactly fire my senses, if you know what I mean.'

'Unlike David,' Carol said, watching her friend intently through the sunglasses perched on her nose.

'Quite.' Turning away, Katarin gestured at the massed trees beside the road. 'The orchards are looking good, aren't they? There are loads of cherries this year. They'll soon be making more of that *Kirschwasser* you enjoyed so much last night.'

Carol made a face. 'Don't remind me.

From now on I'll stick to wine. It's not quite so lethal.'

Without need for any directions from his driver, the pony turned up a tree-shaded lane toward the town and soon they came in sight of pleasant wooded river walks by a watermill whose huge wheel stood silent in a weed-grown channel of the river. Beyond it a bulky round tower gave evidence of the defensive walls that had once surrounded the town.

'That's the wine museum,' Katarin told her friend with a nod at the tower. We'll have a wander round there before you leave, if you're interested.'

'I'm in your hands' came the reply, and 'Do you hear from David very often?'

'No, not often. Our letters have become a bit spasmodic. But he was over for a holiday last year and he may come again at Christmas.' Her blue eyes clouded as she watched the road, where houses closed in on either side with balconies gay with flowers. Most of the houses huddled together, vast gables over windows with bright shutters and bedding thrown out to catch the sunlight.

Carol said, 'You haven't given it up as a lost cause, then?'

'Not exactly.' Katarin sighed. 'It's difficult, Carol. David doesn't believe I'm serious about staying here, though I've told him he could probably get a job in town — maybe with the village council offices. And there's a ready-made home at *Opa*'s if we want it.'

'So you're not prepared to leave?'

'I can't. *Opa* needs me. Anyway, I feel at home here, even if you do think it's a rural backwater. If David wants me, he'll have to come and join me. That's all there is to it.'

'And if he won't?'

Katarin shrugged. 'Then I suppose we'll have to agree to go our separate ways. Things can't go on as they are. We're both in limbo.'

'Well, there's always . . . What did you call him? Berd?'

'Somehow I don't think so,' Katarin said with a rueful smile. 'But tell me about your love life. Who is it now? Paul?'

Carol's mouth curved in a secret smile. 'Paul was months ago. Since then I've found someone . . . someone rather special. Don't be surprised if you suddenly get an invitation to a wedding.'

'What, you?' Katarin said in astonishment. 'But you always said marriage was out for you. You were planning to be a career girl.'

'I know. But maybe I've changed my mind. Don't ask me any more about him,

8

please. I'm scared that if I say too much, it might not happen.'

Blitzen's hooves clopped on, taking the trap into the market square. A huge lime tree, golden with sunlight, spread its branches over one corner outside a gabled Town Hall whose frontage was bright with colored tiles. A covered Renaissance stairway ran up to its upper floor. Opposite it stood a half-timbered house with beams of black and brown beneath a mansard roof, and shops and cafés stood open to a swirl of customers, the square itself sprouting sunshaded tables with traffic passing on two sides.

'Coffee and cream cakes?' Katarin suggested, halting the trap by a trough into which water poured from a bronze fountain.

'I think I can just about manage that,' Carol replied, climbing stiffly down. 'Lord! You'll have to get better springs on that thing, Katie. My back's awfully stiff.'

'You're just out of condition.'

As she stepped down, Bernhard Langren came striding across the cobbles to offer a hand, saying cheerfully, 'Morgen, gnädiges Fräuleins!'

'Well, if it isn't the road hog,' Carol said dryly.

'Ah — you are English,' Berd replied, switching languages. 'You must be Carol.

9

Katti told me you were coming to stay. Allow me to introduce myself — Berd Langren. A pleasure, *Fräulein*.'

Watching Carol dimple as the young man bowed over her hand, Katarin wondered how her friend could flirt with every male she met. Not that she minded for herself. Berd's attentions were becoming a little too determined for her liking and if Carol could divert him, then Katarin would breathe a sigh of relief.

But the respite was only temporary, for Berd swung round and grasped her arm with a possessive hand, smiling down at her with blue eyes that glowed in a tanned face framed by fair, sun-bleached hair. 'You will allow me to buy you some coffee, ladies.'

'Shouldn't you be working?' Katarin asked.

'I should, but since fortune has brought you here on this beautiful morning I shall . . . How do you say? Play hookey?'

At his charming best, Berd escorted them to one of the tables in the square, where he ordered coffee and cakes from a waitress. His heavily accented English seemed to fascinate Carol. She pushed her sunglasses up into her curls and batted her eyelashes at him while Berd played up to this admiring audience and Katarin listened with a wry smile.

'You are very quiet,' he accused her eventually.

'You're doing enough talking for both of us,' Katarin replied. 'Don't worry about me. I'm quite happy sitting here enjoying the sunshine.'

The blue eyes smiled caressingly at her, a breeze lifting a lock of near-white hair at his temple, then his attention flicked beyond her and his eyes narrowed. Glancing round, Katarin saw a sleek black limousine with tinted windows moving slowly through the traffic at the far end of the square.

'The baroness?' she asked, a little shiver raising the hairs on her nape.

'Or her son,' Berd said in an undertone. 'The rumor is that he has returned from America. You have heard, of course, that they have persuaded Friedrich Luz to sell them his vineyard?'

'Yes, *Opa* mentioned it. But Herr Luz is an old man. He couldn't have worked much longer, and he's only got a small patch. He'll be happier with his daughter in Freiburg.'

'That is not the point.' Under the pale hair his eyes were cold as daggers. 'It means the von Drachensbergs own little more of the valley. And next year a little more, and then more, until we are all removed, or working like peasants on land owned by the baron.'

11

'That's ridiculous,' Katarin said.

'Is it? But you do not know them, Katti. Our ancestors were enslaved by von Drachensbergs, slaughtered and maimed. We do not forget.'

'Then it's about time you did,' Katarin said worriedly. 'Those days are long past. There are laws now. And, actually, if it worries you so much, why didn't *you* offer to buy Herr Luz's land?'

'We have not the money. Only the baron can afford to buy. The cooperative put in a bid, but the baron offered more. The death of the old baron has made no difference. This Hugo may be even worse than his father.'

Helping herself to a second cake oozing cream and chocolate sauce, Carol put in, 'You make it sound like the Mafia. Can't we talk about something else? Katarin was telling me about the wine festival, Berd. Are you going to be involved in that?'

He sent a final dark glance after the baronial limousine and turned on a smile. 'I hope so. This year I shall be Wine King, I think. And I shall persuade them to choose Katti as my Queen.'

'You won't!' Katarin almost choked on a mouthful of coffee. 'I'm not eligible. I'm not a native of Gundelheim.'

'You are the granddaughter of Johann

12

Maier,' he reminded her. 'The committee will vote on whichever names are put forward, and I have asked my father to nominate you. You are certainly the prettiest girl in town, and single. The Queen is usually single, though there have been exceptions.'

'Do they vote for the King, too?' Carol asked.

'Oh, no,' said Berd. 'By tradition the King is chosen from among the wine-growing families of the town. Preference is given to a man who is single, strong, and who has not played the role before. This year it is certain to be my turn. If Katti had been a boy, she might have been chosen, so it is appropriate that she should be my Queen.'

'What fun!' Carol said, taunting Katarin with a look. 'What, exactly, do the Wine King and Queen have to do?'

Berd gave her his full attention, becoming eloquent on the subject. 'They ride in a flowered float to open the festival week. They must attend all functions to give their blessing, with their train of followers. And they preside at the ball that ends the *Fest*. After that . . . ' He turned laughing eyes on Katarin. 'The rest is shrouded in mystery. There were once pagan rites to ensure the fruitfulness of the vines in the coming year. Some say that certain Kings and Queens still follow the tradition.'

'Pagan rites?' Carol said, agog with curiosity. 'Such as what?'

'You must ask Katti,' Berd replied, beckoning the waitress to bring the bill. Giving Katarin a sidelong smile, he slid out of his chair and stretched himself luxuriously. 'I must go. I am a working man. Shall I see you soon, Katti?'

'You know where to find me,' she muttered.

As he strode away, Carol watched him with admiring eyes. 'Nothing wrong with him that I can see. He's quite a splendid specimen.'

'And doesn't he know it?' Katarin said sourly. 'I wish you hadn't encouraged him, Carol. I could have done without his company. And what do you suppose your young man would have said if he'd seen you flirting with Berd? I thought you were contemplating marriage.'

'I am. But just because I've seen the goods I want doesn't mean I can't go window-shopping occasionally. Don't you ever look at other men?'

'Well, yes, I look,' Katarin admitted, 'but I wouldn't go any further, not while I still have an understanding with David.'

'What a lot you must miss,' Carol said dryly. 'But what's all this about pagan rites?'

'With a mind like yours I should think you're capable of guessing.'

'Yes, maybe. Rites to ensure fruitfulness.' Smiling to herself, Carol licked her lips in the manner of a cat who scents cream. 'That usually means sex. Did the Wine King and Queen used to go into the vineyards and make mad, passionate love?'

'So they say. By moonlight, apparently. But if Berd thinks I'd join him in that kind of tradition, he's going to be sorely disappointed. Still, I can't see them electing me. I'm not really local. No, they'd never allow that, thank heaven. Come on, let's take poor old Blitzen home. Frau Grainau will be making a start on lunch.'

★ ★ ★

They found the housekeeper busy in the big, airy kitchen, where herbs hung drying in bunches and a solid fuel cooker sent out waves of heat from its alcove. In the courtyard a trestle table stood, laid with a cloth on which a pile of cutlery had been dumped. Katarin and Carol helped carry out fresh loaves of rye bread, egg salad, and cold sausage, with a huge bowl of fresh fruit for dessert and jugs of beer to fill the pewter tankards.

15

'The cellar master will come up and eat with us,' Katarin explained, 'plus Ernst and Gody, who help out wherever there's a job to be done, and anyone else who happens to be around.'

The rambling old house was set back behind the courtyard, with sheds and outhouses holding the presses and machinery. Below their feet the cellars stretched, some formed of the natural caves with which the area was honeycombed.

A high stone wall, hung with creepers, hid the courtyard from the street, and behind the house lay a garden and a paddock where old Blitzen grazed.

The drone of a tractor beyond the wall, followed by an impatient hooting, sent Katarin running to open the gates and allow her grandfather entrance. He grinned widely at her, his flat cap pulled low over a brown face marked by a drooping white moustache. He guided the tractor into a corner of the yard and leaped down to greet Katarin with a kiss.

'Had a good morning, *Liebchen?* And you, Carol, how do you like our valley?'

'It's lovely,' Carol replied.

'We met Berd,' Katarin said. 'He and his father seem convinced that the von Drachensbergs are plotting and scheming to take over the entire valley. That's nonsense, isn't it?'

Johann Maier smoothed his moustache thoughtfully. 'The old baron made no secret of his ambition. Our grapes would improve the Drachensberg vintage, no doubt of it. But Baron Hugo . . . ' He spread his hands and shrugged eloquently. 'Who knows what he will do? It would solve the problem if he joined the cooperative instead of trying to go it alone. But until we find out what sort of man he is, we must bide our time.'

'If I were you,' Carol said, 'I'd go up and beard the dragon in his den and find out exactly what he is planning. Do we eat now?'

Her flippancy was natural, Katarin supposed. A visitor could hardly be expected to understand the centuries of distrust that lay between the baron and the townspeople. Memories were long in Gundelheim.

★ ★ ★

After lunch the two girls walked through the town to the outskirts where, among thickly wooded slopes, a little funicular railway took tourists up to a small café surrounded by mountain walks high above the valley. They climbed aboard the single carriage

17

in company with a score of visitors and found places on the wooden seats. Children scrambled and stared, pointing from the window as the train was drawn up the steep rail with specks of sunlight dropping through a canopy of leaves.

When the train halted, they found themselves deep in the forest, where pathways led in several directions over the humps and spurs of the mountain.

'Shall we walk first?' Katarin asked. 'Or are you ready for a drink? The café's not far.'

'Frankly,' said Carol, 'I think some exercise is in order. What with cream cakes as a midmorning snack and then that huge lunch, you'll make me fat.'

Among the tall trees shafts of sunlight picked out bronze lights on the bark, with the occasional trickle of golden sap. The heady fragrance of pine and larch lay on the air as the two girls wandered, soon finding themselves alone in the forest.

Katarin enjoyed her friend's enchantment with the woods, though she knew that Carol's interest would not last beyond an afternoon. For herself, the forest often provided an escape from the world, a place where she could walk alone and commune with her thoughts and nature.

An involuntary shiver ran through Carol.

'I'm starting to feel cold. It's eerie. So quiet. Where have all the people gone?'

'Up to the café to look at the view, or dispersed along the paths. We'll go back in a minute. I want you to see a favorite place of mine — a waterfall, and a tiny grotto. It's not far.'

The path began to lead downhill, then plunged steeply among a jumble of rocks. Looking askance at the drop ahead of her, Carol shook her head. 'I can't go down there.'

'It's easier than it looks,' Katarin assured her.

'But we'd have to climb back up again. I've no head for heights. I'm tired out already and we've got a long walk back.' She sank down on an outcrop of rock. 'You go, if you like. I need to rest my legs. I'm not used to clambering about in woods.'

Katarin hesitated, torn between the courtesy of staying with her friend and the temptation to go that short way farther to what she regarded as her own private place. Well-marked footholds among the rocks showed that other people did go down to the grotto, but every time Katarin had come this way she had met no one else, so she had begun to feel possessive about the place.

'Are you sure you won't come?' she asked.

19

'There's a marvelous view, and I think there used to be a shrine of some sort, though it's all overgrown now. It has a very special atmosphere.'

'I'm sure it has — for you. No, I'd rather stay here, if you don't mind. You go on. But don't be long in case the goblins come and get me.'

'Five minutes,' Katarin promised, and began to make her way down the craggy path.

Each time Katarin entered the clearing she was overcome with awe at the beauty that lay before her. Pines towered on either side of her and, above, the crag jutted fiercely. From its base, amid a tumble of rocks, the waterfall bubbled in silver streamers, falling for perhaps four feet before it splashed into a cold and sparkling pool that flowed over and down the mountainside.

To one side of the waterfall a niche had been carved at some time in the distant past. Whatever statue it had held had long since vanished and only a few flakes of stone remained among gray-tan circles of lichen. The constant trickle of the waterfall seemed to underline the silence.

When she had first found this secret spot, some instinctive reaction had made her pick a flower and offer it to the water, as one might toss a coin into a wishing well. Now it was a habit. Katarin knelt to pluck a tiny bloom and dropped it onto the surface of the pool, watching as it bobbed for a moment before being swept away.

She knelt there in a reverie, feeling the sun strike warm on her hair and through her shirt, surrounding her with the scent of pine that clung to her clothes. Then some sixth sense warned her that she was being observed and she flung back her head, startled by the sight of a tall man standing on the shelf of rock above the waterfall.

Dressed in a tweed suit with breeches meeting sturdy knee boots, he held a shotgun with casual familiarity. Beside him a huge dog stood poised, watchful eyes fixed on Katarin. Its head came level with the man's waist, and after a moment she identified it as a mastiff, a great muscular beast with drooping ears and pendulous jowls.

Licking suddenly dry lips, she rose nervously to her feet, wondering where the pair had appeared from so suddenly and silently.

'Are you alone?' the man asked in German.

'No. No, my friend isn't far away.' She gestured up the path beside her, disturbed by the oddness of his greeting. Most people simply would have said, '*Guten Tag!*'

'I thought perhaps you were lost,' he said.

21

'No, I'm not, thank you.'

With the crag rearing behind him he looked very much a part of the landscape, ragged dark hair giving him a gypsyish look. The expression on his face was arrogant and stern. Heavy brows drew together above deep-set eyes, though it might have been the sun that made him frown so forbiddingly.

'Well . . . ' she said with an uncertain laugh. 'I'd better go. My friend will be waiting.'

He made no reply, merely stood quietly, watching her. Anxious to get away, Katarin spun on her heel, reaching for a handful of grass to steady herself up the first few feet of the path. Her foot slipped. The rock crumbled under her shoe and her body swung sideways, jarring against the uneven hillside while her knee scraped painfully on a sharp edge of stone. For a moment she hung there, her hand clenched round the tuft of grass, biting her lip to stem an exclamation of alarm.

She was aware of the man lithely climbing down to bend over her. 'Are you hurt?' he inquired.

'No.' Furious with herself, she slithered to a sitting position and examined the tear in her jeans. Beneath it blood oozed from a cut on her knee — not much, but it was sore.

'Serves me right for being so clumsy.'

'Can you walk?' he asked.

'Yes, I expect so. Please don't concern yourself. I'll be fine.'

As he squatted beside her she saw that he had left the shotgun on the rock shelf, where the big dog still stood, head on one side as if waiting for instructions. The man was very close to her, sitting on his heels as he frowned at the blood on her jeans and lifted his head to look directly into her eyes.

The chiseled lines of his nose and jaw were softened a little by a firm, full mouth, and eyes of clear gray looked oddly pale against the deeply tanned face and black hair. Near the corner of his left eye grew a small black mole that in a woman might have been called a beauty spot, but there was nothing effeminate about this man. He was big, broad, totally male.

So close to him, Katarin realized how alone they were in the forest, with no one around except Carol, who probably wouldn't come down even if she called her.

Pull yourself together! she told herself sharply. What do you want to call Carol for? You're in no danger.

Even so, her nerves were in tatters. She scrambled to her feet, brushing at the seat of her jeans, avoiding the steady gray gaze

23

that remained on her flushed face.

'Thank you very much.'

'For what?' he asked. 'I've done nothing.'

'For . . . for being concerned. I'm fine, really. Good-bye.'

Languidly, he rose to his full height, towering over her five feet four. One dark eyebrow crooked slightly in sardonic inquiry, as if he were aware of her disquiet and amused by it. 'Are you sure you can manage?'

'Perfectly sure, thank you.'

She would have liked to depart with dignity, but a desire to get away as quickly as possible turned her flight into an inelegant clamber up the steep and tricky pathway. Hampered by the stiffness in her knee, she hauled herself up around the moutainside until cool shade closed round her and, glancing back, she found herself well out of sight of those disturbing gray eyes.

2

In the ladies' room at the Kienapfel Café, Katarin washed her knee and found that the cut was not deep. At least it had stopped bleeding. Limping slightly, she went out to the veranda table where Carol sat looking at the valley beneath them.

The café had been built on a natural shelf of the mountain, with a steeply angled roof, little balcony, and shutters painted with the pinecone symbol that gave the place its name. In wintertime the café served skiers who came up from the valley, and by night its golden lights were a landmark for miles around. On every side the pines grew in dark-leaved splendor, and behind the café, above the tops of the trees, Burg Drachen was just visible as a pennanted turret. The castle appeared to be averting its eyes in disdain from the common people who frequented the café.

'Okay?' Carol asked as Katarin slid into a chair opposite her. 'You're lucky you didn't break your neck, you know. But tell me about this man you saw. Who do you suppose he was?'

'I've no idea,' Katarin replied, wondering

why she had been so uncomfortable in the stranger's presence. He had done nothing to alarm her, but something about the way he looked at her, coupled with the shot-gun and that brute of a dog, had raised her hackles. 'Anyway, I shall think twice about going to the grotto again, if he's hanging around.'

'You think he was local, then?'

'He didn't look like a tourist.'

'You don't think . . . ' Carol began, and gestured a thumb toward the castle on the crag.

'He could be one of the estate workers,' Katarin agreed. 'Gamekeeper, or something. Maybe even a security man. He certainly gave me the feeling that I was intruding on his territory. Come on, Carol, let's go home. He might turn up here any minute.'

'So what?' Carol asked in astonishment. 'Hey, he really got you rattled, didn't he? What did he do — grab you?'

'No, he didn't. But I had the distinct impression that he was quite capable of it if the mood took him.'

'And you think, he might follow you?' Rolling her eyes, Carol laughed. 'Maybe we should stay. It could be interesting. I'd like to see this mysterious woodsman. Oh . . . It couldn't have been the new baron himself, could it? The actual dragon?'

'No, of course it wasn't. He was much too young. The old baron was in his eighties, so the son must be fifty-odd at least. The man I met was . . . early thirties, at a guess.'

Leaning her elbows on the table, Carol twinkled wickedly. 'Good-looking, was he?'

'You,' said Katarin, 'have a one-track mind. Shall we go and catch the train?'

But, oddly enough, part of her hoped that she might catch a glimpse of the gray-eyed stranger, merely to assure herself that she had imagined the strange vibrations he caused along her nerves. Not because she wanted to see him, to know his name and his purpose. Naturally not.

★ ★ ★

Within a few days it became clear to Katarin that the round of sight-seeing and good food did not entirely satisfy Carol's desire for excitement. In the evenings they sat around the kitchen table over coffee, talking with her grandfather; but though Carol was polite Katarin sensed her restlessness. She kept mentioning Berd Langren as if she hoped to persuade Katarin to seek the young man out for her entertainment, but since Katarin had no intention of offering him any encouragement, Carol had to remain unamused.

On Carol's last day in Gundelheim Katarin took her to the wine museum in the town's ancient gate tower and showed her the traditional but now obsolete wooden presses with their fat, decorative pillars supporting the massive blocks that gave weight to the machines. In an upper room amphorae of earthenware and glass stood on display, reminding people of the Roman occupation of the area. Many vineyard tools had been unearthed, rust-eaten two-pronged hoes lying alongside sickle-shaped pruning and reaping knives, and in glass cabinets stood examples of the colored and decorated wineglasses of the locality.

'This wine business has been going on for centuries, then,' Carol observed. 'I'd never thought about it. I suppose the Romans brought vines so that they could grow their own, to save them having to cart wine from Italy.'

'Yes, they do seem to have been responsible for the rise of wine-making,' Katarin agreed. 'But they say that vines grew here even in the Stone Age. They've been found as fossils. But nowadays the native vines have to be grafted onto the roots of wild vines from America. It's the best way to prevent disease and pests. A hundred years ago the vines in Europe were nearly wiped out by the vine louse.'

'Fascinating,' said Carol, with barely a modicum of interest.

A few other visitors wandered round the cool spaces of the museum, peering at the great wooden vats and tubs, the barrels, and the empty bottles, which showed examples of labelling. Quiet voices murmured around the room and footsteps sounded loud on a polished wooden floor.

'Can we have coffee in the square one last time?' Carol asked.

'That's where I was heading,' said Katarin.

'Good morning,' a deep male voice said in attractively accented English, and Katarin swung round to see the stranger of the woods bending his dark head to look at her through one of the wine presses. 'It's Miss Jameson, isn't it?' he asked.

Astounded, Katarin merely stared, her tongue paralyzed. The man straightened and began to make his way round the press, skirting an arrangement of big brass-bound tubs on his way to join the two girls.

'Who's that?' Carol hissed, but Katarin just gave her a wide-eyed glance. There was no time for explanations with the man in earshot. She could not decide which she felt most strongly — pleasure, fright, or just plain

29

curiosity. The stranger's habit of appearing out of thin air was disconcerting.

He had discarded his hunting tweeds for a linen suit worn with a bright-blue shirt that was open at the neck, casual but elegant. His shoes rapped loudly on the floor as he strode with lithe grace toward them, narrowed eyes fixed on Katarin's face.

'You are Miss Jameson? Herr Maier's granddaughter?' he inquired as he paused three feet away.

'Why, yes.'

'I thought so.' He studied her from head to toe as if noting her simple blue dress and sandals, then ran his glance across the copper-gold hair that fell round her shoulders in waves.

'I'm sorry,' Katarin managed, struggling with a peculiar nervous twitch that made her heart beat erratically. 'Should I know you?'

A faintly challenging smile glimmered in the gray eyes. 'We met on the mountain the other day.'

'Well, yes, but — '

'It was not hard to find out who you were,' he informed her. 'A girl with hair like apricots. An English girl. Your German's very good, but you still have a trace of an English accent. I've heard about you, of course.'

'You have?'

Carol appeared to be enjoying this exchange, looking from one to the other of them with amusement. 'I'm her friend. Carol Masters.'

'How do you do?' he replied gravely.

'You must be the one who scared Katarin half to death,' Carol chatted. 'It took her hours to recover.'

The cool gray eyes flicked back to Katarin's face and he raised an eyebrow the merest fraction. 'If I frightened you, I must apologize.'

'It was nothing of the kind!' Katarin replied with a furious glance at Carol. 'My friend is exaggerating.'

'I trust your knee is better?' he said politely.

'Much better, thank you. So you . . . took steps to find out who I was. May I ask why?'

'I already suspected your identity when we met,' he said. 'You did not appear to be a tourist. And of course I had heard of Johann Maier's English granddaughter, who was studying to be a wine-grower. You're quite famous in Gundelheim, Miss Jameson. For a woman — and a foreigner, at that — to contemplate taking over one of our vineyards, is somewhat . . . startling, shall we say?'

31

'Oh, boy!' Carol muttered under her breath.

Ignoring her friend's undisguised delight in the encounter, Katarin lifted her chin a little higher, her spine stiffening as she returned the man's gaze with a spark of blue fire. 'Actually I'm only half English,' she told him. 'My mother was a native of Gundelheim. And the fact that I'm female is hardly relevant. I passed my exams with flying colors, and I intend to learn all I can from my grandfather. Why shouldn't I run the Maierstufe, when the time comes?'

'Because it is a man's job,' he said with a gesture implying that such an obvious truth hardly needed stating. 'There are no women members of the Gundelheim Wine-Growers' Association. Will a newcomer try to storm the bastions of a centuries-long tradition?'

'I haven't heard anybody else complaining,' Katarin said firmly.

'Perhaps because they don't believe it will happen. Herr Maier, your grandfather, is still a strong and healthy man. Please God he will stay that way for many years to come. And you, no doubt, will find yourself a husband.'

A little hiccup of laughter escaped Carol and she turned away, a hand clapped over her mouth.

Irritated, Katarin found her hands clenched so tightly that her nails were biting into her palms. Spots of color burned on her cheeks, though she wasn't sure which one she was more angry with, her friend or this arrogant stranger.

'I'm the only heir my grandfather has,' she said. 'He's delighted to think I shall keep up the family tradition. What would you like him to do — sell to your master? Is that why you're trying to scare me off? Well, you can go back and tell the baron that if he's got something to say about my plans — my private plans, for my own life — he can come and say it to my face, not send some jumped-up dogsbody to do his dirty work.'

The eyebrow slanted a little higher, his eyes glinting dangerously. 'Dogsbody?' he repeated.

'It means a servant, a man-of-all-work.'

'I'm well aware of the meaning of the word,' the man said in a tone edged with ice. 'I was questioning your use of it to me. I wasn't attempting to 'scare you off,' as you so quaintly put it. I was simply trying to explain how I came to hear about you. Being sidetracked into a discussion of women's rights is probably a consequence of the female habit of grasshopper thinking. But for your information, Miss Jameson, if I did have something to say to you, I wouldn't hesitate to say it to your face. I'm not in the habit of sending servants on such unimportant errands.'

Part of Katarin's mind admired his fluency with the English language, but what she mainly derived from this speech was knowledge of his identity. She cast her memory back, trying to recall how rude she had been, but the words had been said and no power on earth could call them back. She had deliberately insulted the Baron Hugo von Drachensberg.

With a face like graven granite, he made her a small formal bow, said, 'Good day to you, ladies,' and swung on his heel to stride for the door. Even his foot-steps sounded angry, falling swift and heavy on bare boards.

'Oh, dear,' Carol said, trying to hide a smile. 'I assume that was the baron himself. Do you realize you called him a jumped-up servant?'

'He should have introduced himself,' Katarin said crossly. 'How was I supposed to know? I thought he'd be much older. Anyway, if he were a gentleman, he wouldn't have been impolite enough to say what he did. It's none of his business who takes over the vineyard.'

'I do agree,' her friend replied, sparkling eyes swinging to the now-empty doorway, beyond which the throaty roar of a powerful car came noisily. 'He's an absolute chauvinist swine. But he's awfully attractive, don't you think? I wonder if he's married.' Thoughtfully she glanced at Katarin's set face. 'He said you had hair like apricots. It was rather a sweet compliment, when you think about it. And he *was* interested enough to find out about you.'

'Only because he sees me as a threat to his ambitions. He's obviously no better than his father was. I'm beginning to think Berd was right about that. With my grandfather having no male heir, they probably thought it would be easy to acquire the Maierstufe in a few years' time. It *is* one of the major vineyards in Gundelheim. And now I've upset those plans. Honestly, Carol, I don't think I've ever been so angry! How dare he!'

'What a pity I have to leave this afternoon,' Carol said with a mock sigh. 'This could be the start of some real fun. Ah, well, let's go and have some coffee. I'll treat you to a piece of that *Kirschtorte*, or whatever you call it. That should take your mind off the wicked baron and his blue eyes.'

'Gray,' Katarin said flatly.

Sucking in her cheek, Carol made sheep's

eyes. 'You noticed. Dear Katarin, there's hope for you yet.'

★ ★ ★

Soon after lunch Katarin opened the big courtyard gates so that Carol could leave in her small car, heading for Heidelberg, where she would rejoin the three friends with whom she was touring Germany.

'Don't forget to write,' Carol said, leaning from her window. 'Let me know how you get on with the dragon — and with Berd. Hey, you know, that would solve your problems. Marry Berd and let him run the vineyard. That would balk the baron's plans.'

'I shall have to be desperate before I even think of that,' Katarin replied. 'It's been lovely to see you, Carol. Drive safely, now. And don't forget to invite me to that wedding, if it comes off.'

'You'll be top of my list,' Carol promised. ' 'Bye, Katarin. Take care.'

Stepping back against the gatepost, Katarin waved as the car moved off down the twisting street beneath overhanging balconies. The vehicle slowed and stopped not far away and Katarin saw Berd Langren bend to speak to Carol briefly before slapping the roof in farewell salute. Laughing, he waved

36

Carol on her way before ambling to where Katarin was standing.

'So your friend has gone,' he said. 'I like her.'

'She liked you, too,' Katarin replied.

Thumbs hooked in the belt of his jeans, he stood regarding her with soulful blue eyes. 'She is not cool like you. I always find it hard to know what you're thinking, Katti.'

'That's the way it should be,' she replied. 'I'm afraid my grandfather's not here. He's been out all day.'

'I came with a message for him,' he said, helping her close the gates, leaving himself inside the courtyard. 'Tell your grandfather there's to be a meeting of the *Weinfest* committee in the Town Hall tomorrow night. They're going to announce the names of the Wine King and Queen. You'd better come along, too. They'll want to hear you accept the honor.'

'You don't seriously think they'll choose me, do you?' she said in alarm. 'I really couldn't do it, Berd. It should be a local girl.'

'You're local now,' he reminded her.

'Yes, but I'm still an outsider — a foreigner. I've been severely reminded of that only this morning.'

'Oh? By whom?'

'By the Baron von Drachensberg.'

Berd looked as if he had been stung, his whole demeanor expressing shock and suspicion. 'You met him? Where?'

'In the museum,' she replied, startled by his reaction. 'He knew who I was. He'd made it his business to find out about the little English upstart. He was extremely boorish. As far as he's concerned, no woman can run a vineyard, and certainly not an Englishwoman.'

This news made him look decidedly uncomfortable. 'Is that what he said?'

'In as many words. Berd . . . Is it true that people resent me?'

'No, no. Of course not,' he said, much too quickly. 'There are some who think you're overreaching yourself, but everything could change in a few years' time. You'll want to get married and — '

'And raise a family, like a good little girl?' she demanded furiously. 'That's what *he* said. You appear to think we're still in the Middle Ages. If I choose to make a career out of the Maierstufe, then I'll do it. No one can stop me.'

'But if you don't marry,' Berd said reasonably, spreading his hands with a little shrug, 'who will come after you? There's no point in our arguing about it, Katti.

By the time your grandfather is too old to work the Maierstufe, who knows what might have happened? Most of the wine-growers are prepared to wait and see. There'll be time enough to take stands, for you or against you, when you actually come to inherit.'

That was true, Katarin thought. Her grandfather was only in his early sixties and the Maiers were naturally long-lived; her mother's death had been the result of an accident. So *Opa* Maier could live for another twenty years, by which time Katarin might well be married. But she might also have had time to raise her children, leaving her free to follow her chosen career.

'By that time, too,' she said, 'the twentieth century might have caught up with us here. You're right, Berd, it's not worth arguing about. But I assure you I intend to go on learning the business, come hell or high water, husband or no husband.'

'A husband might not let you continue with this career, Katti.'

'The sort of man I might marry,' she said fiercely, 'will understand the way I feel and help me, not hinder me.'

'Like your David?' he demanded. '*Ach was!* He'd never be happy here. You need a German husband.' Still talking in an irritated way, Berd started toward the front gates. 'Whatever the baron said, he had no right to interfere. The Maierstufe is not his concern.'

Something about the tight set of his mouth made Katarin wonder if Berd had a personal grudge against the baron. 'Have you met him?'

'Not recently. Not since we were young.'

'He's not as old as I expected. Somehow, with his father being elderly, I imagined Hugo would be — '

'He's a year or two older than I,' Berd said, his tone and expression eloquent of his dislike of the new baron. 'His father married late in life. The baroness, his mother, was a very beautiful woman, so they say. Perhaps she still is, though few people have seen her lately. And Hugo, of course, has been working abroad supervising their overseas factories. I daresay he will go back to the States when he has settled his father's affairs. It can't be soon enough for me.'

'You're beginning to sound paranoid, you know,' Katarin told him. 'I don't know what you're worried about. He's not likely to sweep down on us with a band of armed cutthroats, the way his ancestors did.'

'Perhaps not, but there are other ways — more insidious ways. If he himself is not here, we shall still have his estate managers and accountants doing his bidding. He's not to be trusted, Katti. Remember that. Now I must go. Don't forget to tell your grandfather about the meeting. I'll look forward to seeing you there.'

When he had gone, Katarin got into her car and drove up the valley to the Maierstufe, where the vines grew in parallel rows interspersed with grassed linkways for ease of access. The grapes burgeoned toward ripeness, hanging in thick green clusters, and among the rows Katarin glimpsed the heads of Ernst and Gody. So close to harvest not much work remained except to keep a sharp eye out for damage from wasps or weather.

Within the next few weeks the harvesting committee would close all the vineyards so that not one grape should be picked before the official date for harvesting. The crop would be left to build up its sugar content, which would be checked occasionally from samples. When the committee deemed the moment just right, the mad rush to pick the grapes would begin. The ripening could not be hurried. It depended on the grapes themselves, on the weather, and on the humidity.

She wandered among the rows checking the fruit for signs of rot and noting the color of the leaves.

'All's well?' she inquired of the bent-shouldered Gody, who nodded and showed stained teeth in a grin.

'All's well, *Fräulein*, though we need some more rain.'

Katarin cast a glance at the nearest fruit, and at the cloudless sky. 'But not too much rain, eh? If there's a storm . . . '

'God forbid,' said Gody fervently, and crossed himself.

Yes, from now on one could only hope and pray, Katarin thought as she returned to her car. She, her grandfather, and their workers had done their best and the rest was a matter for prayer, or luck, however one looked at it. But the weather that year had been perfect so far, just enough warmth and sunlight mingled with a good amount of rain. It augured for a fine early vintage, barring last-minute disasters.

★ ★ ★

When she met her grandfather at supper she learned that he already knew of the *Weinfest* committee meeting, which didn't surprise her. Berd had used it as an excuse to call and see her. Poor Berd. He kept trying, but somehow she couldn't bring herself to respond to his overtures.

'Do you know who's going to be Wine King?' she asked.

He twinkled at her over his white moustache. 'And if I did, do you think I would tell you? It will be announced tomorrow evening. Will you come with me?'

As she had feared, her presence was required, which probably meant that her name was down on the list of candidates for Queen. 'Why, *Opa*? Committee meetings are so boring.'

'Not this one. It may turn out to be quite interesting. Controversial, even.'

The prospect appeared to afford him a certain quiet amusement, and Katarin felt her head grow hot. She knew very well what the controversy would be about — her own nomination as Wine Queen. Most probably a faction would support her out of deference to her grandfather, who was a town councillor, a well-respected burgher, and one of the most important members of the local Wine-Growers' Association; but as she had now discovered, there were other opinions not so favorable toward her.

She recalled the wine museum and a rich male voice saying, 'A woman — and a foreigner, at that.' In a few simple, dismissive words, he had delineated the problems she would face in the future.

Would he be at the meeting? Odd how she thought of him as 'he,' without need for identification in her mind. She had not yet come to terms with the fact that the disturbing woodsman had turned out to be the Baron von Drachensberg. He remained an enigma, a man with cool gray eyes that hid all his thoughts; yet every time he came to mind, which was frequently, she recalled that little tingling of her nerves. In his presence she had felt totally alive, pulse and senses all working in top gear.

For that reason she did not tell her grandfather about her encounter with Baron Hugo.

'If they ask me to be Queen,' she said, 'I shall refuse, you know.' She realized she sounded more certain than she actually felt.

'Shall you?' Herr Maier said mildly. 'Ah, well, we'll see about that.'

* * *

The following evening she and her grandfather went to the market square, to the Town Hall where petunias and nasturtiums grew in bright profusion in pots along the front of the building. A wooden canopy protected stairs that led to the upper chambers, beneath a roof silvery with age and boasting two onion-shaped towers.

Katarin and Herr Maier climbed the stairs to a maze of panelled corridors leading to council chambers and anterooms, with flights of steps in odd corners. In the council chamber itself lacquered oak walls bore the town's coat of arms and official portraits. Old *Bürgermeisters*, magnificently robed, gazed down on the great oblong table surrounded by wooden armchairs, and at one end a few rows of seats held gossiping townsfolk who had come to watch the proceedings. Among them Katarin saw Berd, who beckoned her to join him as her grandfather walked ponderously and gravely toward the anteroom where committee members were gathering.

'I'm glad you came,' Berd said, making room for her on the hard-backed bench. 'It's better to get it all settled at once. If you're chosen, you won't refuse, will you?'

'I'm not sure,' Katarin said.

She still hoped the occasion would not arise, though the more she had thought about it, the more the prospect enticed her. It might be fun to be Wine Queen for a week, presiding at the carnival festivities, even if it meant seeing too much of Berd. In Gundelheim it was deemed a great honor to be chosen, and if it did happen, she could hardly stand up in the council chamber and turn the honor down, not without causing even more ill feeling.

As the committee members filed in and took their places, an air of hushed anticipation rose among the audience, which turned to coughing and shuffling as the meeting began in a mundane manner with readings of minutes. Then Herr Raichle, the *Bürgermeister*, acting as chairman, declared that he intended to break with usual practice and deal with the choosing of the Wine Queen first. A murmur of curiosity ran through the audience, and a glance at Berd told Katarin that he was annoyed at having his moment of glory delayed for unexplained reasons.

It seemed that three names had been put forward for the role of Wine Queen, but one girl had withdrawn because she would be away for festival week. Which left Annchen Griebel — a pretty blonde girl whose family and friends occupied half the benches, smiling and nodding at the candidate — and Katarin Jameson. When her name was announced, Berd took her hand and squeezed it, while someone from behind leaned to wish her luck. From all she could gather, no one really objected to her inclusion.

The twelve members of the committee

46

wrote their choice on slips of paper. Those went into a velvet bag, which was passed back to the chairman, who counted them out into two piles.

'There are eight votes for Katarin Jameson,' he announced, seeking her out across the length of the room. '*Fräulein* — you accept?'

'Stand up!' Berd hissed.

Katarin did so, on legs that felt like jelly, and heard herself say, 'I'd be delighted. Thank you.'

The listeners applauded, even her rival's family seeming only slightly disappointed, while Annchen herself smiled and waved at Katarin. She was only eighteen. There would be other years.

Katarin sat down again, too bemused to take in what she had done. Her grandfather had said there might be controversy, but it had all passed very smoothly.

'That's good,' Berd was saying, a smug grin on his face as he soothed his fair hair. 'We'll enjoy ourselves, Katti. It's a pity your friend Carol will not be here to see us.'

Clearing his throat, Herr Raichle called for silence and everyone settled down to hear the name of the Wine King announced. The *Bürgermeister*, a fat, fluffy-haired man, looked round at the faces of his committee

47

with a frown of uncertainty.

'Are we agreed?' he asked.

'Yes, yes,' one man replied impatiently, and another said, 'Why not?' But Georg Langren, Berd's father, sat with folded arms looking like a thundercloud and Katarin felt Berd's tension. Something had gone wrong with his plans.

'It has to be me!' he said under his breath. 'Who else is there?'

Herr Raichle looked up and addressed the gathering. 'It has been decided, for the sake of tradition and good manners, that the role of Wine King shall be offered to Baron Hugo von Drachensberg.'

'What?' Berd exclaimed, loud enough to be heard by everyone. All heads turned in his direction and he leaped to his feet, scarlet in the face. 'You can't do that!'

'It has been decided,' the mayor said sternly. 'His family is one of the oldest in Gundelheim, they are wine-growers, and the baron himself is single, healthy, and has not been chosen before — mainly because he has not been resident here. He is therefore eligible, and the committee — most of them — feel that it would be polite at least to offer.'

'He'll never do it,' someone said in a bored voice. 'Sit down, Berd. It's your year.

Everyone knows it.'

Assuming a careless attitude, Berd sank back into his seat and smiled at Katarin rather forcedly. 'They're stupid even to make the offer. He'll laugh at them. He wouldn't lower himself to join in our fun and games. He's too proud for that.'

'Then why have they suggested him?' she asked.

He shrugged. 'As they said — old tradition. And maybe someone wants to ingratiate himself. I've never heard anything so foolish.'

The meeting continued with discussion of details of the festive week, and finally broke up with the serving of coffee in an anteroom where smoke and loud voices filled the air. Most people commiserated with Berd, declaring the choice of the baron a mere courtesy that would come to nothing. 'Just tugging the forelock,' one man said cynically.

Katarin found herself surrounded by people wishing to shake her hand and congratulate her, and if undercurrents of resentment existed she could not sense them. Everyone seemed genuinely pleased to regard her as part of the community.

'Well, Katti,' her grandfather beamed, forcing a way through the crowd to join

49

her. 'Not so boring, was it? I knew you wouldn't refuse when the time came.'

'I'm still not sure I should have been nominated,' she replied. 'You didn't put my name down, did you?'

'You can thank Georg Langren for that. I voted for you, of course. You'll be the most beautiful Queen we've had in years.'

'Thank you, *mein Herr*,' she replied with a smile, not believing it. 'But who was it suggested the baron as Wine King?'

'Herr Raichle himself. He feels we should show our gratitude to the baroness for her kindness to the town, which isn't much appreciated, unfortunately, but she does help out in many quiet ways. She's a fine lady. When you think of it, her son is the most obvious choice.'

'You agree?' she said in astonishment. 'But everyone says he won't do it, so isn't it an empty gesture?'

He tapped her arm in the way he had when he wished to gain her full attention. 'It's the offer that's important. Between old Baron Heinrich and the town there were certain tensions. We want to show Baron Hugo that the past is forgotten. We wish to offer the hand of friendship and this seems as good a way as any. No, he won't do it, but he will realize what it means. We

50

shall take him a flag of truce, you and I.'

Swallowing thickly, she croaked, 'You — and I? You mean . . . '

'Why, yes. We shall go up to the castle and tell him what happened tonight. Since you are Wine Queen-elect and I a committee member, it will be appropriate. He's only a human being, Katti. He'll be flattered, especially when the message is brought by such a charming young woman.'

Flattered? she thought with an inner groan. He hadn't been very flattered by the names she had called him in the museum. She had certainly not been 'charming' that day. But perhaps he would be gentleman enough not to remind her of that in front of her grandfather.

3

Herr Maier telephoned the castle and on saying that he wished to see the baron on a matter concerning town business, received an invitation to present himself at Burg Drachen the following Sunday afternoon. Unfortunately he developed a severe cold and was confined to bed when the day came.

Katarin despaired of her luck. As a rule her grandfather enjoyed good health, but now when she needed his support a hacking cough and high temperature prevented him from accompanying her. She could hardly ask Berd or his father to give her moral support since the committee's decision had infuriated them. Herr Langren seemed to feel that an insult had been offered to his son, and though Berd pretended sanguinity, Katarin knew how resentful he was.

So she went alone, using her grandfather's BMW sedan.

The road to the castle led up past the little railway station and curved past acres of vines, becoming steadily more steep and twisting through a band of scrub where foxgloves lent a cerise tint to the hillside. Eventually the narrow way writhed up past the conifer line, with legions of firs marching on either side as the road levelled out, rounded a final curve, and she came in sight of the gate arches behind which the castle loomed gray and forbidding.

The archways bore ornate carvings, though the edges of the sculpture had been blurred by the weather of centuries. Beyond them lay a broad paved courtyard where Alpine shrubs bloomed against the ancient walls and ivy twisted round the foot of a wrought-iron balustrade that guarded the stairs to the front door.

Two cars stood in the courtyard, one a silver Mercedes-Benz, the other a Porsche with customized paintwork done in shades of pink and bearing a scrolled letter *F* on the doors. His and hers, Katarin thought, though she couldn't imagine the baroness driving around in a pink Porsche and, besides, her name was Anna. Who might *F* be?

Parking the BMW unobtrusively in a corner, she climbed out to look at the castle, feeling that she had been sent on a fool's errand. She wore a neat gray suit with the jacket unbuttoned to display a lime-green blouse with a slim bow decorating its round neckline. Since it was a Sunday and the visit fairly formal, she had swept her hair up into a knot on her crown, leaving a few curling ends round her face. She thought of it as understated elegance, and it gave her the courage to climb the worn treads of the stone steps to the imposing arched porch that sheltered the doorway.

As she stepped onto the porch the door opened and a manservant dressed in black bow tie and dark suit greeted her in appalling German. He was obviously English, but she thought it more polite to let him carry on using German. Or was it? Suddenly light-headed with nerves, she stepped into a vast hallway.

A grand staircase lay ahead of her, surrounded by statuary and suits of armor, while to one side an expanse of parquet flooring led to deep carpets on which stood low chairs and settees, with more armor and statues guarding deep window niches. Stags' heads glared balefully down from either side of an enormous stone fireplace.

'This way, please,' the butler said in his garbled German. 'The *Herr Baron* is expecting you.'

'Thank you.'

She followed him up the sweeping staircase, wondering if the baron was in fact expecting his visitor to be the young woman he thought

54

unfit to run the Maierstufe.

More steps led up to an alcoved door, where the butler knocked and went in, saying, 'The lady from Gundelheim is here, sir.'

'Lady?' the familiar baritone repeated. 'Well, show her in, Smithson.'

Opening the door wider, Smithson gestured her into what was obviously a study, lined with books and watercolor paintings. One corner opened out into a tower whose leaded windows looked over the valley, and on the padded seat beneath the windows lounged a slender girl dressed in electric blue, with dark hair done in a braid falling across one shoulder. Hugo von Drachensberg stood by a stone fireplace, leaning on the wall, looking taller and more dangerous than ever in an all-black outfit of shirt and slacks.

For a moment he didn't move, his gray eyes flicking over her in swift appreciation; then he eased himself away from the wall and advanced with outstretched hand, regarding her with that maddening quirk of one eyebrow.

'Why, Miss Jameson,' he said in English, quite calmly. 'This is a pleasure. I was expecting your grandfather.'

'He . . . he's not very well, I'm afraid,' she faltered, accepting his handshake under the haughty stare of the girl in the windowseat. 'So I came alone.'

'Demonstrably,' he said.

'Hugo . . . ' The vividly blue-sheathed girl shifted in her seat, asking what was going on, and with a gesture of apology he switched smoothly to German.

'If you don't mind, Fräulein Jameson, we will speak in my language. Franziska is not very familiar with English. Oh, excuse me — may I introduce you to Franziska Bader-Wehr?'

So this was *F* of the pink Porsche, Katarin thought, extending a hand. '*Wie geht es?*' she said. 'How are you?'

The girl replied with a limp handshake, a withering look, and discounted Katarin. She was very young and very beautiful, Katarin thought, with skin like porcelain and liquid dark eyes, but it was a cold sort of beauty and the scarlet mouth looked sulky.

'I thought you said it was town business,' Franziska pouted at Hugo. 'One of the burghers, you said.'

'That's what I was told,' he replied, not taking his eyes off Katarin, who felt the color creep up to stain her cheeks. 'Perhaps you'll explain, Fräulein Jameson?'

'I . . . ' Now that she was here, the mission seemed even more crazy. She took a deep

56

breath and said in a rush, 'I was asked to come and inform you that the *Weinfest* committee would be honoжed if you would be Wine King this year.'

The swift widening of his eyes was the first unguarded expression she had seen on his face, but her attention switched away from him as a hiss of indrawn breath came from Franziska. The girl stood up in one slinky motion and moved closer to Hugo, laying a possessive hand on his arm. Her skin looked white against his black shirt, and scarlet nails stood out like drops of blood, while her eyes darted scorn.

'Are you mad?' she inquired of Katarin. 'Do you know whom you're speaking to? What a ridiculous idea! The *Herr Baron* would not demean himself to play such silly games. Wine King, indeed!'

'Whose idea was this?' Hugo asked. There was little change of expression, but his eyebrow tilted a tiny fraction and Katarin fancied she saw a humorous gleam in his gray eyes. Her worst fears had come true: he was laughing at her.

'I believe Herr Raichle suggested it,' she murmured, 'though the whole committee agreed.'

'Ah, the good *Bürgermeister*,' he observed.

'The man should be stripped of his office,'

Franziska said, flicking her braided hair behind her shoulder. 'It's an insult.'

'It was intended as an honor!' Katarin said hotly. 'Though no one ever expected the *Herr Baron* to do it. I was merely asked to come and make the offer. I've done that. Now I'll go back and tell them — '

'Wait!' The order rapped out from Hugo as she turned away. 'Let's not be hasty about this. It *is* an honor. One I never expected, especially when I've been away so long from Gundelheim that I might well have been accused of deserting my old friends.'

Not believing her ears, Katarin turned to face him and saw that Franziska had drawn back and was regarding him with equal disbelief.

'Hugo!' she breathed. 'Surely you would not think of — '

'Why not?' he asked.

Clenching her hands, Franziska shook herself in petulant anger and whirled on her heel to march past Katarin to the door, where she paused to say, 'You are both mad! If you do this thing, Hugo, I shall never speak to you again!'

The violent slam of the door seemed to echo around the castle as Katarin found herself alone with the Baron, who appeared unmoved by Franziska's threats. He watched

Katarin levelly, waiting for her to speak.

She, however, was so astounded that she could think of nothing to say. He couldn't be serious, she kept thinking. If he became Wine King, with herself as his consort, they would have to be together at all the functions during festival week. Thinking that Berd was to be her King had been bad enough, but if Hugo took the part instead . . . Her mind couldn't grasp the concept.

'You seem surprised,' he said. An understatement, she thought, since she could feel herself gaping like a goldfish. 'Why don't you sit down, Miss Jameson? We must talk about this.'

His gesture led her into an armchair of brown leather, deeply buttoned and extremely comfortable, as she discovered when she sank into it. It was also rather low, so that when Hugo strolled toward her she had to throw back her head to look him in the eye. His glance strayed over her raised chin and the soft curve of her throat with an appreciative gleam that brought back her nervousness. She looked away from him, toward the window, and arranged her skirt to cover her knees, brushing at a nonexistent speck of fluff on the material.

'I've forgotten exactly what happens at the *Weinfest*,' he said.

'They, er . . . ' She cleared her throat and tried again. 'They'll send you a full program, I expect. If you really mean to accept.'

'They expect me not to?' He sat down on the sturdy coffee table in front of her, putting himself more on her level, leaning with one arm braced beside him. From the gleam in his eye she guessed that he found the whole thing diverting. 'I like to do the unpredictable at times,' he told her. 'Don't you, Miss Jameson? Will they be as surprised as you were?'

'Yes, I'm sure they will be — but delighted, of course.'

'Oh, of course.' All of a sudden he laughed so naturally that a shiver of delight ran along her spine. In this mood he was very attractive. 'Shall I make a good Wine King, do you think?'

'I'm sure you'll be excellent, *Herr Baron.*'

'Wine King. Better than being a jumped-up dogs-body, no?'

A fresh flush made her eyes look blue as lilacs before she lowered them in shame. 'I meant to apologize for that. I had no right to speak to you in that way, even if you hadn't been . . . who you are.'

'The *Herr Baron,*' he said gravely, though a deep note of amusement still lurked in his voice. 'Must we be so formal, Katarin?

My name is Hugo. Tell me, is the Wine Queen chosen yet, or do I pick my own? I've forgotten how it's done.'

'They take a vote on nominations. The meeting was last Thursday.'

'And?'

She had hoped he would not ask, but he had to know. Sighing heavily, she lifted her head. 'They elected *me*.'

'Ah,' was all he said, but his eyes danced with laughter and his mouth twitched.

Disconcerted by the way her heart had begun to pound, she stood up, brushing down her skirt, straightening her jacket. 'I'm glad it amuses you. Are you sure you know what you're doing? Wearing funny costumes . . . presiding over dancing and feasting . . . doling out wine in the square . . . It's hardly your sort of thing, is it? Do please think about it seriously. If you take it on, you have to go through with it.'

'I intend to,' he assured her. 'Especially now.'

'Now?'

'Now that I know I shall have you to assist me,' he said, and eased himself to his feet, smiling wickedly down at her.

Thoroughly flustered, she turned away.

'Won't you stay and have a drink?' he asked. 'Some tea, perhaps? Smithson makes an excellent pot of tea.'

'Thank you, but I'd better go. I've left my grandfather in bed. He'll be expecting me.'

He accompanied her from the room, all gracious politeness, though she sensed that he was still laughing inwardly. She was torn between vexation and the desire to respond to his good humor. His unexpected acquiescence would surely astound the worthy burghers of Gundelheim.

Then with a pang of disquiet she remembered Berd. Berd wasn't going to be pleased at all!

As they descended the great staircase a female figure dressed in a black skirt and white blouse, with befringed silk shawl round her shoulders, stepped into view and watched them with curiosity. She wore her graying hair drawn up and back into a soft bun and leaned heavily on a stick. Although no longer young, Hugo's mother remained an attractive woman who carried herself with dignity.

Reaching the hallway, Hugo performed formal introductions and Katarin made contact with the baroness's warm hand, and with her sharply assessing eyes, which were gray like her son's but lacking his humor.

'I've just been told about this proposition,'

she said. 'Hugo, you can't mean it. To be Wine King ... It wouldn't be dignified for a man in your position. Think of Franziska's feelings. If she has to watch you cavorting ... '

'She isn't obliged to watch,' he pointed out. 'And who says the Wine King can't be dignified? I've no intention of 'cavorting,' Mother, or drinking myself into a stupor. I'm sure Katarin would not be pleased if I did. We shall bring a new dimension to the festival. Joy, merriment — and sobriety.' He slanted a grin at Katarin. 'Within reason, of course.'

Unable to restrain an answering smile, she glanced aside to where Franziska had appeared, her face a study of displeasure. 'What do you mean 'we'?' she demanded. 'What has she to do with it?'

'She is to be my Wine Queen,' he replied.

She shook herself angrily, all but stamping her foot in childish temper. 'I shall be humiliated! Oh, it's too much, Hugo! I shan't allow it!'

'Allow?' he queried in an ominously quiet voice. 'I don't recall asking your permission, Franziska. You are free to go right away and not witness any of this, if you find it so offensive. Personally, I intend to enjoy every minute of it.'

'O-ooh!' she spluttered, 'You're impossible! *Baronin*, speak to him! Tell him he's being ridiculous.'

The baroness shook her head ruefully. 'That will do no good. I warned you he would prove hard to tame. Like his father. All the von Drachensbergs have a willful streak.' She turned her head to smile at Katarin. 'Think yourself fortunate, Fräulein Jameson, that you will only have to put up with him for a week. Poor Franziska is intending to take him on for a lifetime.'

This casual remark stunned Katarin. For a moment she felt detached, as if cocooned from her surroundings. Hugo planned to marry that spoiled child? What on earth had possessed him? But another glance at Franziska told her clearly enough what possessed him — the girl's youth and beauty. Perhaps he enjoyed having someone to dominate.

He led her to the door and came with her down the steps to where she had left the BMW, though she protested that such a courtesy was not necessary. When she climbed into the car and tried to close the door he prevented her, leaning on the door to look at her.

'Drive safely, Katarin. The mountain road's tricky. And please give your grandfather my best wishes. I hope his health improves very soon.'

'You're very kind, *Herr Baron*,' she murmured.

'Hugo,' he amended.

'Hugo, then. Thank you. If you'll just let me close the door . . . '

'I shall see you very soon,' he said, making her look full at him in surprise.

'Shall you?'

'But of course,' he said with a slow smile. 'There'll be things to organize, won't there? We must discuss how we shall tackle this project. Maybe between us we can make this the best *Weinfest* Gundelheim has ever seen.'

He closed the door before she could reply, which was probably just as well, for she hadn't known what to say.

★ ★ ★

She found her grandfather dozing, though he roused himself when she arrived. Having been told the news, he lay staring at her speechlessly for a while, saying eventually, 'This may mean trouble, *Liebchen*. Berd will not be pleased.'

'That's what I thought,' Katarin said with a sigh. 'But there's nothing he can do about it. He'll just have to wait another year.

Really, it serves him right for taking so much for granted. If he hadn't gone to so much trouble to get me elected Wine Queen, just so that he could have an excuse to hang around me . . . Now he's hung with his own rope. And I can't say I'm sorry. His attentions are getting a bit embarrassing. Heaven knows what might have happened during festival week, with a few glasses of wine inside him.'

'It was not jealousy I was thinking of,' her grandfather said, a troubled look in his eyes. 'Not that sort of jealousy, anyway.'

'Oh?' Worried, she sat down on the end of the bed.

Her grandfather stirred, glancing at the window. 'Is it raining?'

She nodded. 'It started as I came down the mountain. That's just what we needed for the grapes.'

'Yes, it's good.' A gnarled hand plucked at his quilt. He looked very tired lying there propped up by pillows, his eyes reddened by the effects of his cold.

'Can you tell me about it?' she asked. 'About Berd and Hugo? I've suspected there was something personal in it. Berd gets much too hot under the collar whenever the baron's name is mentioned. His father, too.'

'It was a long time ago, Katti,' he replied.

'They were both boys. I never got to the truth about it, but the Langrens have never forgiven or forgotten. If you want to know more, you must ask Berd.'

She sat silent for a moment, thinking about that. What could have happened between two boys that would still cast a shadow now?

'You'd better go and phone the *Bürgermeister* and tell him that his offer has been accepted,' her grandfather said. 'It will be up to him to inform the committee. For myself, I would not like to be the one to pass on this news to the Langrens.'

Katarin had been worried about the same thing, but since Herr Raichle had started this whole business he could have the pleasure of breaking the news. 'I'll do that right away,' she said. 'And then I'll make you a hot drink.'

That night, before she went to bed, she stepped out onto the small balcony outside her room, protected from a soft drizzle by the overhanging gable. Below her the lights of Gundelheim twinkled and there came the sound of music from a nearby inn. From a corner of the balcony she could just see the dark shape of Burg Drachen looming on its hilltop. Low clouds sent a drape of mist to drift across the castle, so that a single visible light there seemed to fade and brighten. Did the light come from Hugo's study? she wondered.

In her mind she could picture the room quite clearly, a quiet masculine retreat with that attractive tower corner, full of books. Full, too, of the vital personality of the master of the castle. How brown his skin had looked against the black shirt, with a pulse beating softly in his throat and that tiny mole drawing attention to brilliant gray eyes full of laughter. Just remembering it caused her stomach to jerk with guilty pleasure, and for the first time she admitted to herself that the woman in her had responded irresistibly to the man he was.

But the knowledge brought her no comfort. Hugo von Drachensberg was not for her. Even if Franziska had not existed, his rank and title, not to mention his wealth, put him way out of Katarin's reach.

With a final glance at the light in the castle, she sighed and retreated into her room, firmly closing the window in the same way she closed her mind to impossible dreams. Or tried to.

★ ★ ★

It rained, gently and steadily, for three days, and each time Katarin went up to the vineyard the grapes looked plumper and riper. Her grandfather began to recover from his cold, much cosseted by Frau Grainau, and Katarin spent her time in the cellars with Fritz Kurtze, the cellar master, and his assistants, cleaning out the glass-lined vats and oaken wine casks, and sharpening the vine-cutters that the pickers would use when harvesting began. Everything had to be sparkling clean, from the great presses in the outhouses off the courtyard to the mashing machines and the network of pipes that would pump the grape juice from one process to the next.

One afternoon Katarin found work in the smaller of the cellars, where her grandfather kept his special wine that was not sent off to be handled by the cooperative. With the new vintage about to be made, it seemed a good moment for reorganizing the bottles.

Because of the natural chill in the cellar, she wore a thick jersey with her jeans as she tenderly moved bottles to fill a rack. Since her grandfather grew mainly Rülander grapes, his wine was full-bodied, with a delicate bouquet and a pale color that darkened to golden-yellow with age. Finer wines existed but few could compare with the Rülander from the Maierstufe of Gundelheim.

'Katti!' came Berd's voice from above.

69

She sighed to herself, wondering what mood he would be in. 'Down here. Berd.'

As he thumped down the stone steps, she continued with her work, not looking round until he demanded, 'What did you say to him?'

'Say to whom?' she asked in surprise.

'Hugo von Drachensberg! You know who I mean! What made him agree to be Wine King?'

A flush stained his fair skin beneath the pale blond hair and a nerve jumped in his cheek below blue eyes darkened by anger. Katarin felt herself stiffen, ready to defend Hugo.

'He appreciated the honor. You see, he's not as proud and standoffish as you said he was.' Turning her shoulder to him, she took another bottle from the rack and moved away.

'What wiles did you use to persuade him?' Berd demanded.

'Don't be ridiculous.'

'Look at me!' he shouted, grabbing her shoulder to spin her round.

The bottle flew out of her hands to smash against the foot of a nearby rack, spilling its precious contents across the stone floor. Katarin stared at it in horror for a moment before wrenching free from Berd's grasp, rubbing at her shoulder.

'Now see what your stupid temper's done!' she flared at him.

He gave her a shamefaced glance, his mouth set. 'I'm sorry. I'll clean it up for you.'

'That's not the point, is it? What right have you to come here shouting at me? I know you're disappointed, but don't take it out on me.'

'I'm sorry,' he said again, and reached for her, spreading his hands in appeal when she backed away. 'Katti, forgive me. I've only just found out, from someone in the street. No one thought to tell me officially.'

'Didn't Herr Raichle — '

'No one.'

'Oh, Berd . . . I'm sorry. No wonder you're upset.'

He turned away, scratching at the back of his head. 'When did you see him?'

'Last Sunday.'

'And what happened?'

'Nothing happened. I gave him the message and he seemed to think it was a fine idea. Berd . . . he doesn't know that you were hoping to be Wine King yourself. Don't blame him for this.'

Giving her a bleak glance, he whirled and slammed the side of his fist into the wall with

71

all his strength. The blow must have hurt him but he gave no sign of it. 'It's always the same! He has everything, and still he takes things from me. Now he will be Wine King instead of me, and . . . ' He stopped, looking at her as an idea had just struck him. 'You can let Annchen be Queen. You can find some excuse. Say you're too busy. With the harvest coming up you'll have no time to play Wine Queen. After you've studied so hard it would be unreasonable to expect you to miss the most important time.'

'Oh, no, Berd.' She shook her head stubbornly. 'I've accepted and I'm going to do it. It won't take up all that much time. Don't ask me to tell lies.'

His expression coarsened with disgust. 'You'd rather be with him than with me, wouldn't you? Well, wouldn't you, Katti?' One stride brought him close to her and he locked his hands round her arms, backing her up against a rack full of bottles.

'Stop it, Berd!' she cried, alarmed by the fury in his eyes.

Seeing his intentions, she twisted her head away as he bent toward her, so that his mouth met the side of her chin, fastening there a moment before he stepped away and released her.

'I've tried every way I know,' he said with

a gesture of futile anger. 'But you're cold through and through. Your friend Carol would not have refused me. *She* is a real woman.'

'Then go and find someone just like her!' she exclaimed. 'I'm sorry, Berd, really I am. I just can't feel that way about you. Why can't we go on being friends, the way we've always been?'

'Because that isn't enough anymore! Very well, I can wait. Enjoy your week as Wine Queen. And remember that Hugo von Drachensberg wouldn't look twice at you. He's amusing himself, that's all. You know he's spoken for?'

'I don't see what difference that makes!' she cried. 'We're just going to preside at the *Fest*, in full view of the whole town. Anything else is in your nasty mind.'

'Or his,' he said with a curl of his lip. 'Just remember he's not to be trusted.'

With that, he marched away and stamped back up the stairs. Katarin rubbed her chin in distaste, trying to remove the unwelcome feel of his lips. She hadn't needed reminding that Hugo was unattainable; she remembered it every time she looked up at the castle.

He had promised that she would see him very soon, but there had been no sign of him. Well, of course there hadn't! She hadn't really expected him.

That evening she wrote to David, a bright letter full of news. A little desperately she asked if there was any chance of his coming over soon as there were things they needed to discuss. She signed it with love, out of habit, though David had begun to seem very distant, like a fading picture that brought back nostalgic memories of something long past. But perhaps if she saw him again, it would be different. Perhaps he could save her from doing something stupid.

★ ★ ★

A further blow awaited her when she came in one evening to find that the Wine Queen costumes had been sent from their store in the Town Hall. She had seen them before when previous Queens had worn them, but she had not looked closely enough to realize how old and tattered they were. The costumes comprised two full-length shifts made of cotton, one a pale green like ripened grapes, the other intended to be white, though in fact it was more gray. With them came a thin purple cloak, a crown of simulated vine leaves, and a belt hung with bunches of plastic grapes.

After supper she tried the green gown on

to show it to her grandfather in the hope of helpful suggestions. The dress was simply made of two pieces of material with seams at the shoulders and down the sides, leaving openings for her head and arms. When she put it on, her slip showed quite clearly and obviously she would need an underdress of some kind, for modesty if not for warmth.

Fitting the vine-leaf crown on her head, with her hair flowing loose around her shoulders, she stood in front of her full-length mirror and scowled at her reflection. The Wine Queen would need to use her ingenuity if she were not to look like a ragtag peasant.

'Katarin!' her grandfather called from below. 'Katarin, come down here a moment.'

'I'm coming.' With the faded dress floating round her, she went lightly down the stairs to the sitting room, saying, 'Just look at this, *Opa*. What on earth do you — ' and stopped, dismayed and yet delighted by the sight of Hugo von Drachensberg rising politely from the settee.

'The *Herr Baron* has called in to see me,' her grandfather told her proudly. 'Look — he has brought me a bottle of cognac, to cure my cold.'

'How kind of him,' Katarin said faintly, transfixed by the half-smile that curved

Hugo's mouth as he took his time in studying her appearance. At last the brilliant gray eyes returned to her face, which she knew must be bright red. She was virtually standing there in her underwear.

'Fit for a Queen?' Hugo said, a little frown between his brows. 'It hardly fits at all. Mine is just as bad.'

'I suppose they have to cater for all sizes,' Katarin babbled. 'Last year's Queen was quite, er . . . '

'Rotund?' he said with a laugh. 'Yes, I've seen some in my youth that looked like sacks of potatoes. But you, Miss Jameson, are slender as the Lorelei. And if you wear that thing, you may catch pneumonia.'

'I'll go and change,' she muttered, and fled.

Hurriedly throwing on a shirt and jeans, she brushed out her hair and paused to catch her breath, wondering why she felt as though she had run a mile. Her heart hammered, her face burned, and her eyes gleamed unnaturally bright. Just because *he* had come.

'Slender as the Lorelei,' she thought. He certainly knew how to pay a pretty compliment. In reality the Lorelei was a rock that stuck out into the river Rhine and threatened shipping, but in legend — the

76

way Hugo had meant it — the siren named Lorelei had lured men to their doom with her beauty and her song. The comparison was deliciously flattering.

And he had come, just as he had promised. The cognac for her grandfather had been a convenient excuse. She was sure of it.

'Now stop that,' she ordered her reflection. 'Don't start imagining things.'

4

Hugo did not stay long, and for most of the time he talked with her grandfather about the prospects for the harvest and about the town in general. He seemed interested in catching up with events that had happened during his absence in the States.

Katarin indulged herself in relishing the sight of him and listening to his voice make dark music as he talked. He seemed entirely relaxed, chatting and joking, long legs stretched out across the rug and a hand occasionally gesturing to emphasize a point.

She contributed a small share to the conversation, a little more as time passed and she became convinced that she was not imagining his personal interest in her. Excitement knotted inside her every time he glanced at her, for his eyes seemed to hold private messages that said he must be sociable with her grandfather, though really he would have preferred to be alone with her.

Part of her recoiled in guilty shame, realizing the wrongness of responding. Franziska stood as an unseen presence between them, and there was David, too. But however guilty Katarin felt, her attraction to Hugo was stronger. Neither of them, she felt sure, would allow the pull of their senses to overrule propriety, so where was the harm?

When he took his leave, she went willingly out to the courtyard with him, knowing she was taking a further risk. But a few private words could hardly constitute a major sin.

The rain had stopped and the August evening remained mild, calling up a mist that would benefit the grapes. Overhead stars gleamed through fronds of flying cloud, and a streetlamp sent golden light across half the yard before the wall cut it off, laying deep shadows where a Virginia creeper stirred in the night breeze.

Just outside the house, Hugo paused, breathing deeply of the evening air as he threw back his head to look at the sky. 'It's a fine evening. They forecast a spell of dry weather. It looks good for the harvest.'

'*Opa* says it may be a bumper year,' she agreed. 'Thank you for coming. He was very pleased. And it was kind of you to bring the cognac.'

'I couldn't come empty-handed,' he said, looking sidelong at her. 'I did tell you I would see you soon.'

'I remember.' Her heart raced, sending

blood rushing through her veins, making her feel breathless. 'Where did you leave your car?'

'Outside.' Slowly, he began to walk toward the gates, with Katarin beside him as if drawn by a magnet. 'Those costumes are terrible,' he added. 'It's time the town had some more. I think I'll offer to replace them, if I can get someone to make new ones in the time we have left. Four weeks, isn't it?'

'The *Weinfest* begins four weeks next Saturday,' she replied. 'It looks as though it may clash with the harvest. It will be a hectic week. Hugo . . . '

His smile told her he had noted her use of his first name and approved of it. In front of her grandfather she had addressed him more formally.

'Yes, Katarin?'

'Do you know Berd Langren?'

'I used to. It's a long time since we met. Why do you ask?'

'I wondered. He's . . . a bit upset. He expected to be Wine King himself this year.'

He made no reply, but in the shadows thrown by the wall she fancied she saw him frown. 'I didn't know.'

'I know you didn't. It's all Herr Raichle's fault. But I thought you should know. Berd has a hot temper. Not that I think he'll make trouble — not really trouble. But you may hear some mutterings.'

'I see,' he said gravely. 'Yes, I understand. Thank you, Katarin.'

'I just thought you ought to know,' she said again, too tense to think clearly. They were alone, in almost darkness, stars overhead and light from the house slanting out onto the courtyard, not quite reaching them.

Lifting a hand, Hugo stroked a lock of hair back behind her ear and let his wrist rest on her shoulder while he looked down at her in the shadows.

'Tell me something,' he murmured. 'When we met in the woods that day, what were you wishing for?'

'Wishing for?' she breathed with a little nervous laugh.

His fingers moved softly through her hair as if enjoying its silky texture. 'The way you were kneeling, with your head bent, making a sacrifice to the gods of the mountain . . . '

'It was just a wildflower.'

'But the intention was there. That's why I came up quietly, so as not to startle you. You looked . . . like a supplicant. Sad. Wistful. Wishing for what, Katarin?'

Embarrassment flooded her as she realized

how easily read her actions had been. She had thought often of that day, when she had wished for something unnamed and he had appeared. But she could hardly tell him that he himself was the answer to her prayer. The old gods enjoyed irony. They had sent him, but they had made him unavailable.

'That's my secret,' she said.

His free hand came up to touch her face, making her tremble. 'You won't tell me?'

'You must allow a girl a few mysteries,' she said lightly, and when he cupped her face between his hands, lifting it to his, she caught her breath, muttering, 'You shouldn't. Please, Hugo . . . '

Very slowly, he let his hands fall, saying in a low voice, 'You're right, of course. I shouldn't. But I want to. And so do you.'

'That's no excuse,' she said wretchedly. 'You're not free, and . . . and neither am I. We shouldn't indulge ourselves when other people may be hurt.'

He straightened himself, putting more space between them. 'There's a man in your life?'

'Is that so surprising?'

'No. No, of course not. I hadn't

thought . . . Is it Berd Langren?'

An unsteady laugh choked out of her. 'No, it isn't. It's . . . He's an Englishman, actually. I don't see him very often. I suppose I'm lonely, and you . . . you're very attractive.'

Vaguely, she saw his mouth curve in a wry smile. 'Thank you for that. But forgive me, Katarin. We'll be friends. We can do that.'

'Yes, I hope so.'

He turned away to open the gates and she stood watching as he climbed into the silver Mercedes, lifted a hand in farewell, and roared away up the road. Shaken by the intensity of feeling that blazed inside her, Katarin closed the gates, resting her head on the cool metal for a moment as she fought against a rush of hot tears. The moment Hugo had touched her she had known that no man before had ever had such an effect on her. Not even David. It was clear to her now that whatever she had felt for David had withered and died long ago.

'He's a fine young man,' her grandfather said when she returned to the sitting room. 'So natural. Not like his father. Baron Heinrich was always condescending, too aware of his title. Why, if you didn't know better, you'd thing Baron Hugo was one of us.'

'Well, he is, isn't he?' Katarin replied. 'Just a man like any other.'

'Perhaps so. But he is also a baron, Katti. He is very rich and influential.' Pausing, he gave her a look from the corner of his eye. 'I hear he's engaged to be married.'

So he had noticed the undercurrents, had he? That was hardly surprising since he was far from stupid and knew her too well, but she had thought she was being discreet. Obviously she must be more guarded from now on.

'Yes, he is,' she said casually. 'Her name's Franziska Bader-Wehr. I met her when I went to the castle. She's very beautiful.'

'Bader-Wehr,' he mused, stroking his moustache. 'Yes, it would be an appropriate match. Her family, too, is an old and wealthy one. From the Rheingau. They have big vineyards, though Franziska's father is a politician. Such an alliance can only bring more prestige to both families.'

'Then it's fortunate that the *Herr Baron* and his fiancée are so much in love,' Katarin said. 'Is there anything you want, *Opa*? I think I'll get to bed.'

'No, nothing for me. I'll have another glass of this excellent cognac and then I'll come up myself. Good night, *Liebchen*.'

She lay in bed trying not to think about Hugo while she relived every moment of his visit, her skin burning at the memory of his touch. It was madness. It was wrong. But, oh, it had been thrilling!

★ ★ ★

Only a couple of days later a woman arrived to measure Katarin for new costumes, much to her surprise. Hugo must have moved with speed, and to judge by the woman's comments, she was delighted to oblige the baron with her services as a needlewoman.

'He knows exactly what he wants,' the dressmaker told Katarin. 'Don't you worry, the costumes will be ready if I have to sit up every night to finish them.'

Exactly what designs she planned she would not divulge. She took Katarin's measurements and with more reassurances she left as suddenly as she had arrived.

★ ★ ★

The days slipped by. In the Maierstufe, grapes ripened under the sun, their sugar content improved every time a sample was tested. Sugar turned to alcohol during fermentation, and a high sweetness meant an excellent prospect for the wine.

For Katarin herself, nothing seemed to be going right. Several times she sat down to attempt a letter to David — a truthful letter that would tell him she no longer loved him, but without hurting him. The right words eluded her, however, and she kept finding herself out on her balcony staring up at the castle.

She began to think herself hopeless where men were concerned. Distance had blighted her love for David; Berd's admiration had only embarrassed her; and she had known from the start that Hugo was beyond reach.

Even playing Wine Queen had become a prospect to fear, for during that week she would be constantly in Hugo's company, with all the dangers that entailed. For him, perhaps, a brief romantic fling might be amusing, adding spice to the festival, but since Katarin could not take her relationships lightly, it was best not to contemplate even a flirtation.

All she had left was the Maierstufe, and the vines.

Shopping in the market one day, amid canopied stalls laden with groceries and household goods, she was preoccupied in trying to remember everything she needed to buy. A heavy basket dragged on one hand and the crush seemed intolerable as people pushed and jostled while market traders called their wares.

A hand suddenly closed over hers, relieving her of some of the weight of her basket, and she turned in surprise to find Berd smiling at her.

'Let me help,' he said. 'You look hot and tired, Katti. May I buy you a cup of coffee?'

She relinquished the basket, glad to be rid of the load as she squinted at him in the sunlight, though she was puzzled by the change in his manner.

As if he guessed her thoughts, he grimaced. 'Why should we quarrel? It's stupid. I hope you can forgive me for what I did. I would like to be friends again.'

'Yes, so would I,' she said. 'Friends, Berd.'

'I ask no more. I've been in a terrible mood lately, because of the way I was treated over the Wine King business, but that's over now. I don't care who does it. It's all foolishness, anyway, and when it's done it will be done. One week, and then everything will return to normal.'

'And there's always next year,' she reminded him.

He feigned indifference. 'Oh, I've stopped caring about it. Let Hugo von Drachensberg have his little game. I know very well what he's doing.'

'And what's that?'

'Trying to charm the town. Trying to make everyone forget that he aims to rule this whole valley some day. Didn't I tell you he would use underhanded methods? But it won't work. He'll only make a fool of himself.' Slipping a hand round her arm, he led her toward the edge of the crowded market. 'Let's see if we can find a couple of seats in the *Gasthof*.'

'So, Katti,' Berd said when they had been served. 'Have you heard from your friend Carol?'

'I don't expect to. She's not much of a one for writing letters.'

He spooned sugar into his cup, watching the swirl of liquid. 'She seemed to enjoy her stay. Will David be coming soon? It must be over a year since he was here.'

'He may come at Christmas,' she said, wondering at the trend of the conversation.

'It's a strange relationship,' he mused. 'Doesn't he like the idea of living over here playing second fiddle to the Maierstufe?'

'That's none of your business,' Katarin said. 'And unless you want us to quarrel again, I suggest you change the subject.'

'Very well.' Stirring his coffee, he stared across the room. 'You had a visit from our local aristocrat, I hear.'

'Where did you hear that?'

'Oh, news travels fast in a small community like this. His car was seen outside your grandfather's house. Besides, your grandfather told my father that the baron had deigned to pay him the courtesy of calling. To inquire after his health, so he said.'

Although she knew he was leading up to something, she could not imagine what it might be. The memory of Hugo's visit came back vividly, making her feel on edge. No one could possibly know about that guilt-ridden few moments in the dark courtyard, but she herself could not forget it. She feared that Berd might read the truth in her face.

'And so what?' she demanded. 'Is there some law about someone paying a neighborly call? He didn't stay long.'

'Long enough to set tongues wagging. It was not very discreet of him, but then a man in his position thinks himself above gossip. He wouldn't care what interpretation people might put on it.'

Baffled, Katarin felt irritation run along her skin like ants after sugar. 'I don't know what you're talking about, Berd. What are you trying to say?'

'Only that you should be more careful. Everyone knows that you are single and unattached — your David is so far away he doesn't count. So when Baron Hugo starts to pay calls at your house, whatever his excuse may be, people put two and two together.'

'Oh, really!' she exclaimed. 'I never heard such nonsense. You seem to have forgotten that he and I are both involved with plans for the *Weinfest*. Of course we shall have to see each other. It's ridiculous to suggest there's any more to it.'

'I'm only warning you that rumors are starting. So far it's a joke, but you're a pretty girl and everyone knows that Hugo von Drachensberg never could resist a pretty face. There was a girl he brought home from America one time — a real beauty. And a magazine ran an article once, telling about all his love affairs in New York.'

'Newspapers blow everything up out of proportion,' she replied defensively. 'It would be strange if there had been no women in his life. That must have been before he became engaged.'

'Among the upper classes such things make no difference,' Berd said, his mouth twisted. 'Marriages are made for profit, and the partners go their own ways. They all have affairs. It's the thing to do. The girls of Gundelheim are fair game to him. It was the same with his ancestors. Nothing changes.'

'That's malicious gossip!' Katarin said hotly. 'You've got absolutely no proof of it.'

'Then you don't care if people say he's added you to his list of mistresses?'

About to explode, she calmed herself for fear of causing a scene, saying in a low, angry tone, 'What are you trying to do, Berd? Turn me against him in order to ruin the festival? Why do you hate him so much?'

'Who said I hated him?' he countered.

'It's obvious. And since you haven't met him for years you ought to be ashamed of yourself. If he did something against you, when you were both boys, isn't it time you forgot about it? You're both adults now. Whatever it was, it's in the past.'

His lips had thinned, his eyes staring through her as if he looked at bitter memories. 'Some things you don't forget. I know him better than you. The von Drachensbergs are all from the same mold — all scheming, greedy, ruthless . . . He'll take the valley if we let him. He'll use every means in his power, and not care who gets hurt in the process. Just be careful you are not one of

91

the casualties, Katti.'

Slamming some money down on the table, he took his leave of her. Katarin, troubled, sat and finished her coffee, thinking about what he had said and the motives behind it. Something had happened in the past to turn both Berd and his father against the von Drachensbergs, and now they were repeating all sorts of damaging things about Hugo. And none of it was true.

Or was it simply that she did not wish to believe it?

Berd had to be wrong, she decided. But unfortunately the suspicions had been planted and refused to go away.

★ ★ ★

She received an invitation to attend one of the planning meetings at which details of the *Weinfest* celebrations were to be arranged. When the day arrived she walked down to the Town Hall in a mood that veered between apprehension and elation. Hugo would be there; she knew that even before she saw the silver Mercedes parked on the market square, but the sight of the car, confirming his presence, made her heart leap. As she climbed the steps beneath the wooden canopy, her palms were damp.

The side room seemed to be full of people, some perched on tables while others stood in groups, many of them making notes. Representatives of dancing groups and bands mingled with inn owners and committee members as they discussed the program of events.

But the whole gathering dwindled to a background hum as Katarin's eyes met luminous gray ones across the room and she knew he had been watching for her. Her pulses jumped in reply, unsettling her.

'Ah, Fraülein Jameson, there you are.' The fuzzy-haired mayor materialized beside her, shaking her hand before leading her across the room. 'Have you heard the news? The *Herr Baron* has promised us a haunch of venison as well as an ox to roast in the square. It promises to be a festival to remember. Ah, *Herr Baron*, you know Fraülein Jameson, of course. Yes, of course. Stupid of me. It was she who persuaded you to do us the honor of being our Wine King. For which we are eternally grateful to her. And to you, of course.'

Herr Raichle burbled on, while Katarin and Hugo bade each other a formal good evening and shook hands. His eyes smiled at her, saying he was glad to see her, and his fingers pressed a little more tightly than was necessary. For the life of her she couldn't concentrate on what the mayor was saying.

The meeting proved a lengthy, tortuous affair. Katarin had no choice but to remain near Hugo, since any instructions for him necessarily included her. The Wine King and the Wine Queen would appear everywhere together, except on the Friday night of the festival, when a rowdy men-only event took place in one of the beer cellars, an equivalent of a 'stag night' that celebrated the bridegroom's last moments of freedom.

Only then did it strike Katarin that the whole *Weinfest* symbolized the union of the male and female parts of the vine. She had known it, but had not considered that aspect before. Processions and feasting on the first Saturday would be followed by solemn ceremonies on Sunday, signifying the meeting and betrothal, then during the week various festivities celebrated the people's joy in the coming 'marriage' — the final grand ball on the second Saturday. In modern times it was all done in fun, naturally, but it promised to be a week fraught with painful undercurrents with herself and Hugo in the vital roles.

The room seemed to get stuffier as she contemplated the emotional hurdles ahead, and she was not sorry when at last the meeting broke up. Even then, as if by chance, she found herself close beside Hugo as people called, '*Gute Nacht*,' and car doors slammed.

'Where did you leave your car?' he asked.

'At home. I walked down.'

'Then let me give you a lift.'

'Thank you, but it's a pleasant evening. I can walk.'

'I know you can walk,' he said softly. 'I wish to save you the trouble. If you're worried what people will think, they'll probably think more if I go without you.'

And if she stood and argued with him, she thought, there would be even more cause for gossip. 'Very well. Thank you.'

The Mercedes was very comfortable, the seat of gray suede molding to her body. Katarin laid her head against the rest and closed her eyes, trying to clear her mind, trying not to feel excited because she was alone with Hugo.

'You're tired?' he asked as he turned the key and the engine purred into life. 'You look pale this evening. Aren't you well?'

'I'm fine, apart from a bit of a headache. It was hot in there.'

'You must take care of yourself,' he said. 'I don't want my Queen to be ill.'

'Maybe it would be for the best.'

'Don't say that! You aren't serious, are you? You're not getting sick?' He sounded genuinely concerned.

'Not as far as I know,' she said. 'No, don't worry. I'll be there.'

Being so near him was sweet torture, and she sighed to herself in regret when the car slid to a halt outside the big gates that led to her grandfather's house.

'Katarin . . . ' Hugo said softly. She felt a warm hand on her wrist, causing her to jump like a startled kitten as she looked round at him. In the soft light from the dashboard she saw the amused lift of his eyebrow. 'You're nervous,' he observed.

Her taut nerves snapped in face of his teasing. 'Of course I'm nervous! You know very well . . . You promised . . . I can't play that sort of game, Hugo. It's fine for you — you can do anything you like. But *I* have to live down here. I have my reputation to think of. Just because your ancestors took their pleasures when and where it pleased them, you shouldn't — '
She stopped, horrified by the words she had never meant to speak, and by the coldness that wiped all amusement from his face.

'Good night,' she choked, and leaped from the car, running to fumble with the gate handle.

She gained the courtyard and was about to close the gate when Hugo's hand stopped her; his strength preventing her from shutting him out. Not believing her senses, Katarin stepped back, her thoughts darting frantically. What was he doing? Had he gone mad?

He caught hold of her and swung her round so that her weight made the gate creak shut. 'Since you choose to accuse me of bad intentions,' he growled, 'I may as well give you cause.'

'I didn't mean it!' she gasped. 'I don't know what made me say it. Hugo, please . . . '

One arm locked round her waist, pulling her full against him, while the other hand lifted her chin despite her struggles. 'What is it you say in England?' he said through his teeth. 'Might as well be hung for a sheep as a lamb?'

'Please don't — ' The gasp was cut off abruptly as he kissed her, making her head spin even while she attempted to fight him off. He was all harshness, his hold on her brutal and unrelenting, heat radiating from his body to engulf her while his mouth made savage demands.

Struggling forlornly, she beat at him with her fists, but as he continued to hold and kiss her strange fires began to leap inside her. Part of her mind still protested, but its voice grew weaker as her physical self responded to him.

With a tiny groan she gave in to the clamor of her senses. Her mouth melted against his and her body became pliant, allowing him to press her closer to the firm warmth of him. His name repeated in every beat of her blood as she realized that his fierceness was no longer a product of anger. Caught up on a wave of longing, she fastened her arms round his neck and returned his kisses, further aroused by the way his hands ran over her back and tangled in her hair.

'Katarin!' he murmured hoarsely, pressing his lips across her face to her ear and throat. 'Katarin!'

Through the heady fog of desire, Berd's words whispered insidiously in her head: 'He's amusing himself. The girls of Gundelheim are fair game for him.'

'No!' she cried, and with an effort wrenched herself free of Hugo, shame and suspicion warring inside her.

In the deep shadow of the creeper-hung wall, he stared at her as if dazed, his breathing sounding hoarse and quickened. He reached a hand toward her, saying, 'Katarin, forgive me.'

'Robber baron!' she flung at him, and the hand dropped as if she had bitten it. 'Now

I know what Berd meant. He said you had everything, but still you took more. What sort of man are you, anyway? Isn't one woman enough?'

He drew himself upright and through the shadows his voice sounded harsh. 'Is that what you think of me, or are you Berd Langren's echo?'

'I can only judge by your behavior,' she said, close to tears.

'As I judge by yours,' the reply came, bitter with disgust. 'Will you claim the blame is all mine? Are you that much of a hypocrite?'

'No.' She was shaking with misery. 'No, perhaps I've given you reason — '

'Perhaps?' he broke in with a sharp laugh. 'You've been throwing yourself at me since the moment we met. How could any man refuse such a clear invitation?'

She felt as though she had been slapped, all her romantic dreams vanished on the cold wind of reality. What he said was not entirely true, but that he could say it at all proved what an idiot she had been.

'Go away!' she cried. 'Just go away. And if ever you touch me again — '

'Don't worry about that.' His voice came chill. 'I assure you that before I come near you again you'll have to go down on your knees and beg me.'

She heard the clash of the gate and he was gone, driving off into the night, back to his lair on the mountain. Katarin flung her hands over her face as the tears came hot and uncontrollable, despair slicing through her. He was hateful. He was cruel. He was all the things Berd said of him and worse.

So why did she feel so wretched?

5

Fortunately her grandfather had gone out that evening, so he was not there to witness her distress. She could never have explained to him what she didn't understand herself. This thing with Hugo, whatever it was, had flared too suddenly for comprehension. She hardly knew him, after all, and yet he had come to dominate her thoughts and her emotions more thoroughly than any man before.

Grimly she applied herself to her work, spending long hours in the vineyard and the cellars. When evening came she was so tired that she went early to bed and slept despite the sick pangs of longing that assailed her whenever she thought of Hugo. The more she turned over in her mind what had happened, the more she felt that it had been her own fault. Perhaps she had made her feelings too obvious, but it had been done in innocence, not calculatingly, as he had implied.

★ ★ ★

Hugo's involvement with the *Weinfest* appeared to be producing results. The citizens of Gundelheim, naturally polite and formal, referred to the head of the von Drachensberg family as the *Herr Baron*, but slowly Katarin began to hear him called 'Baron Hugo,' the name spoken with pride and affection. She remembered how Berd had said that Hugo was trying to charm the town, and that did appear to be what was happening. Certainly fewer people mentioned his suspected ambitions toward the valley, but whether Hugo had cold-bloodedly planned for this effect or whether it manifested itself simply as a by-product of his genuine interest in the coming festival she could not decide.

Despite everything, she remained hopelessly drawn to him, if only in her mind. Never, she vowed, would she give him the satisfaction of knowing she was half in love with him.

However, if she had thought that she would not see Hugo again until the festival, she had underestimated him. To begin with, he telephoned and invited her grandfather to look over the castle vineyards and give his opinion. Herr Maier, obviously flattered, went gladly, returning to tell Katarin all about it.

'No wonder they don't do so well,' he said.

'The soil is too rich over on Burg Drachen land and it's my opinion they're growing the wrong sort of vine. Baron Hugo seemed pleased with my advice. We had a long talk with his overseer and I believe they will make certain changes.'

'If he wanted advice, he had only to go to the Wine-Growers' Association,' Katarin said, wondering why her grandfather's visit to Hugo's vineyard should disturb her so much. Was it because she felt excluded?

'I'm a member of the association,' Herr Maier reminded her. 'They'll be pleased he called me in. For too long the von Drachensbergs have kept to themselves. Obviously it hasn't done them any good. Their yields are poor. A combination of bad planning and ill-advised cellar management.'

'Is that what you told him?' she asked in astonishment.

Smiling, he stroked his moustache. 'Not exactly. I was more diplomatic, but I've asked him to come and see the Maierstufe. He might learn better from example.'

'Did you suggest he might join the cooperative?'

'I mentioned it. It's a case of planting ideas subtly, Katti. One doesn't tell the baron how to run his business. But despite that he did listen to what I had to say. He's a young man who will not close his ears to the voice of experience.'

But Katarin could not help but wonder why, out of all the wine-growers in the area, Hugo had chosen her grandfather as his adviser. She could have named three or four other men with an equal amount of experience and knowledge.

★ ★ ★

A few days later she came in from the vineyard to find the silver Mercedes parked sociably in a corner of the courtyard.

'My grandfather has a visitor?' she inquired of Frau Grainau in the kitchen.

'The *Herr Baron*,' the housekeeper confirmed with pride. 'They met somewhere in the town, it seems. Now they're down in the cellars with Fritz.'

'I see.' At least she was relieved that Hugo was not in the house, so if she was careful she need not meet him. Presumably he would leave when he had made his tour of inspection.

'Everything's prepared for supper,' Frau Grainau said. 'The fish is baking in the oven and the onions are steaming. You'll just have to sauté the potatoes in a little while.'

'Fine. Thank you.'

Fetching her coat, the housekeeper buttoned it across her ample bosom, her eyes alight with curiosity. 'Shall you invite him to stay for a meal? It's good of him to take such an interest, but we're beginning to expect such things of Baron Hugo. He's not a bit like his miserable old father. Why, he spoke to me very kindly, as if he was really pleased to meet me.'

'Yes, he does have excellent manners,' Katarin said.

She went up to her room as soon as the housekeeper had gone. From there, while she washed and changed, she kept an eye on the courtyard, listening for the men to come up from the cellars.

Aware that supper would be almost ready, she was about to venture down to the kitchen when she heard her grandfather's voice in the courtyard and saw him gesture toward the house, obviously inviting Hugo to come in. Hugo, wearing a formal dark suit and white shirt, smilingly accepted, much to Katarin's chagrin. She dodged out of sight in case he should look up at her window, her heart fluttering with indecision. Should she go down and brave it out, or should she stay in her room and hope her grandfather would think she had not yet come home?

She was hovering on the landing, listening to their conversation, when her grandfather suddenly stepped into the hall below.

'Ah, there you are, Katti,' he said. 'Come down and say hello to Baron Hugo. I've just been showing him the cellars.'

'Yes, I know,' Reluctantly she made her way down the stairs. Her grandfather must not suspect there was anything amiss.

He was entertaining his visitor with a bottle of his best wine in the comfortable window alcove of the kitchen. Appetizing smells filled the kitchen. Katarin cast one glance in Hugo's direction, avoiding his eyes.

'Good evening, *Herr Baron*,' she murmured. 'You'll excuse me if I continue cooking. *Opa*, why don't you take the *Herr Baron* into the sitting room? The kitchen is hardly the place for a visitor.'

'On the contrary,' Hugo said smoothly. 'It's very pleasant in here. It smells good.'

'You're welcome to join us for supper,' her grandfather said, sending Katarin into a panic that expired on a breath of relief when Hugo replied that he was expected back at the castle.

'But this wine is really excellent,' he added, accepting another glass. 'Such a beautiful color and bouquet.'

'The Maierstufe has always produced the

best wines in the valley,' her grandfather said smugly. 'Now that Katti has been trained in the latest techniques, we look forward to further improvements. Don't we, Katti?'

'We certainly do,' she replied firmly, remembering how Hugo had derided her ambition.

As she laid the table she was aware of him on the edge of her vision, a dark-clad figure lounging in a low chair by the window, and she knew that he was watching her even though he continued chatting with her grandfather. She flashed him one cool glance and met expressionless gray eyes that didn't even flicker. His only reaction was to tilt an eyebrow mockingly. She could have slapped his arrogant face. He had come here simply to torment her.

'I'd better not outstay my welcome,' Hugo said. 'Your grandaughter's anxious that your supper shan't be spoiled, I expect.' Draining the last of his wine, he stood up.

'Oh, there's no hurry,' Herr Maier protested. 'The food will keep for a few minutes. Have another glass.'

'I won't, thank you, though I regret having to refuse such a remarkable vintage. But I have to drive, and I shall be in trouble if I'm not home soon. My mother was expecting me much earlier.'

'Perhaps she would enjoy a bottle of our Rülander,' Herr Maier said. 'I'll send her one.'

'I'm sure she'd be delighted,' Hugo murmured.

Knowing that she must behave more naturally, Katarin forced herself to look at him again. 'I hope your mother's well?'

'Very well, thank you, Fräulein Jameson,' he replied gravely.

'And Fräulein Bader-Wehr?'

His eyes held no readable expression, but a corner of his mouth lifted into a sardonic little smile. 'Franziska is as beautiful as ever.'

'Ah,' said her grandfather. 'Have you set a date for your wedding yet, *Herr Baron*?'

'No, not yet. I shall let the lady do that when she's ready. She has many commitments.'

'Of course. Of course. Forgive me, I didn't mean to sound impertinent. Katti, go and open the gates for Baron Hugo.'

Glad to escape, she went out to the courtyard where the late sun slanted, turning her hair to pale flame. Behind her Hugo took leave of her grandfather and strode across to his car while Herr Maier watched from the doorway, beaming.

The Mercedes maneuvered across the yard

before heading for the open gates, where Katarin stood. Its near window slid down as it drew alongside her and stopped, though Hugo kept his gaze on the dashboard.

'I gather the costumes for the festival are coming along well,' he said.

'Oh, good,' Katarin replied.

Hugo squinted up at her. 'It promises to be an interesting week, don't you think?'

'Very interesting,' she agreed, her chin high, though her insides churned. She remembered all too clearly the way he had kissed her on this very spot, and the hurtful things he had said.

'Are you still angry with me?' he asked.

'What do you think?' she retorted.

Bitterness twisted his mouth and suddenly the engine roared to life. The car shot out onto the road, leaving her with a spatter of gravel from the courtyard and the satisfaction of knowing that she had put him in his place. Except that it gave her no real pleasure. His visit had only reminded her of how unhappy she was.

Oddly enough, though she was sure that her grandfather had noticed at least some of the tension between her and Hugo, he said nothing about it. In fact he avoided mentioning Hugo's name all evening.

★ ★ ★

After that Hugo found a dozen reasons for calling at the house, either to ask Herr Maier's advice or to bring something to show him. He treated Katarin with a distant ambivalence that infuriated her even while she replied in kind.

Frau Grainau seemed thrilled by all the attention her employer received from his illustrious 'pupil,' and no doubt she went gossiping about the town with the story, but Katarin was convinced that Hugo's behavior was not as innocent as it seemed. She spent most of her time feeling like a coiled spring, winding tighter and tighter every time she encountered him.

On a sunny morning only ten days before the *Weinfest* was due to start, she drove up to the Maierstufe in the pony trap, giving Blitzen some exercise. Every day now the harvesting commission examined the grapes in order to make a final decision on the date when they would declare the vintage. There was little to be done except wait, but Katarin could not stay away from the vineyard. She felt a personal interest in this year's results now that she had passed her exams and become a fully fledged viniculturalist.

As the pony clopped up the road a blue car

110

came in the opposite direction. Berd's car, she saw. He slowed and stopped as she drew level with him and she reined Blitzen in.

'It's looking good for the harvest, then,' Berd said, leaning from his open window. 'It will probably be the same week as the *Fest*. How are you going to do both jobs?'

'I shall manage, I expect,' she replied. 'What have you been doing with yourself lately? I haven't seen you.'

'I didn't think you wanted to see me, especially now you've got so thick with Hugo von Drachensberg. He's at your house so often I wonder you don't charge him lodgings.'

'He comes to see my grandfather,' Katarin said flatly. 'He barely speaks to me.'

'Does that bother you?'

She tossed her head, making the ribbons flutter on her hat.

'Not in the least. Quite frankly, I wouldn't care if I never saw him again.' Clicking her tongue, she slapped the reins to urge Blitzen on up the sloping lane, her temper smoldering. Only with an effort had she stopped herself lashing out at Berd. His jealousy was an irritant, but not half so maddening as Hugo von Drachensberg could be when he tried.

Driving the trap along one of the grassed

linkways that crossed the Maierstufe, she left Blitzen to graze while she wandered among the rows peering at the grapes, occasionally picking one to enjoy its sharp sweetness. It would be a bumper year, she thought with a little thrill of pride.

Then she saw dark clouds gathering from the direction of France and a frown creased her brow. The forecast had warned of rain, but those clouds looked ominous. To her alarm a low mutter of thunder ran along the horizon. Oh, no, not that! A storm now could ruin a whole year's work.

At that precise moment she heard the Mercedes, coming the long way round from Burg Drachen. By now she knew the exact note of the engine so well that the very sound of it raised her hackles. What demon prompted him to intrude on her peace every day? If he didn't soon give up, she would be forced to say something, even if it meant upsetting her grandfather.

Craning above the serried rows of vines, she glimpsed the top of the silver car as it came down the lane, and to her annoyance it stopped by the gate leading to the grassed avenue where she had left the trap. Damn him! she thought, clenching her hands as she saw Hugo come out of the car and approach the gate.

She could always hide among the vines, but that would be too ridiculous. She had suffered too many humiliations to bear another, though at least this time there were no witnesses.

Balancing her hoe in one hand, she strode back to the linkway, a slender figure in shirt and jeans with her hair flowing behind her and the ribbons in her straw hat streaming valiantly in the breeze that had sprung up. Hugo waited for her, dressed all in dark blue — slacks, shirt, and jacket matching perfectly, hands in his pockets and his head slightly on one side. As she marched nearer to him, she saw that sardonic eyebrow twitch into a hook. It served as the final turn that broke the coil spring of her temper.

'Just what do you think you're playing at?' she demanded furiously. 'Who gave you permission to come here?'

The eyebrow lifted a fraction more. 'Your grandfather did. He said I could look round the Maierstufe at any time.'

'Unaccompanied? You should know that isn't done, especially just before harvest. This is private land.'

'But I knew you were here,' he said with a gesture to where the trap stood some distance away. 'I thought perhaps you might show me round.'

'I don't have the time. And don't look so innocent, Hugo! I know what you've been doing. You're deliberately making a nuisance of yourself, hanging around my grandfather, pestering me everywhere I turn. I won't have it! Why don't you just . . . just go away and leave us alone?!'

In her temper she waved the hoe menacingly, causing him to look genuinely alarmed. 'Be careful!' he exclaimed, throwing up a hand as he stepped out of the way.

'Careful? I'll brain you if you don't stay away from here!' She lifted the hoe as if intending to strike him with it, though she knew she could never do such a thing.

Mouth compressed, eyes blazing, he stepped in under the hoe and laid firm hold of it, twisting it from her grasp with one flick of his wrist. 'Don't threaten me unless you mean it!' he growled.

'I did mean it!' Katarin cried, rubbing at her wrenched wrist, too furious to think straight. 'Oh, you're . . . you're hateful! I detest you! Go away.'

He tossed the hoe to the ground and stepped grimly toward her. She retreated, throwing out her hands to ward him off.

'Don't you dare touch me! Stay away!' Terrified, she spun round and began to run, hardly noticing that the sun had blinked out.

Overhead dark clouds swirled and boiled, shot through by lightning.

A cry escaped her as Hugo's hand fastened on her arm and he whirled her round to face him in the peculiar yellow-tinged light that presaged the storm. Both of them were breathless, both angry.

'Don't dare me, Katarin,' he warned in a low voice vibrant with rage. 'I always take dares as a challenge.'

Glaring at him through her lashes, she pulled ineffectually against the immovable hand locked round her wrist. 'You're hurting me.'

'And so? Who began the violence today? Not me, for sure. I came in friendship.'

'No, you didn't! You came to annoy me.'

'Why should I do that?'

'Don't ask me! It probably amuses you. Everything amuses you, doesn't it? Playing Wine King. Patronizing my grandfather.'

'Katarin!' he said in exasperation and jerked her toward him, throwing his arms round her as he said her name again in a quite different tone. 'Katarin . . . '

'Don't do that!' she gasped, squirming, but he only held her tighter. She kept her head down, her face pressed to the dark-blue shirt as she muttered insults. 'Pig! Brute! Bully! Let me go!'

His arms felt warm and strong around her and he laid his cheek on her hair, saying again, 'Katarin . . . Oh, Katarin . . . '

All her muscles were taut, her hands clenched against his chest, her eyes squeezed shut in an effort to stop the stupid tears that wanted to pour out. Every breath brought the scent of his body, the warm clean odor peculiar to him and fragranced with a whiff of tangy cologne that brought back memories of earlier encounters.

Her misery erupted in a great sob, followed by more that shook her body as she huddled in his arms, wanting to fight him off and yet unable to move.

'No, Katti,' he said anxiously. '*Liebling*, don't be so upset. Please . . . ' He forced his hand beneath her chin, lifting her face. She resisted stubbornly, but at the last moment her willpower deserted her and she reached toward him, finding his mouth with an intensity that drove out everything else. Her arms slid round him, holding him with all her strength as the flames of passion flared between them, threatening to consume her.

A crash of thunder directly overhead made no impression on her until she felt the deluge that followed it. She and Hugo sprang apart as the skies opened and drenched them. Water stormed down like steel rods, battering

116

the vines that surrounded them.

Gasping under the onslaught, Katarin stared in disbelief, shivering, with her shirt plastered wetly to her. Hugo threw off his jacket and attempted to put it round her, but she battered at him with her hands, crying, 'The grapes! The grapes!'

'There's nothing you can do!' he shouted above the tumult. 'Come to the car. We must get under cover.'

'No!' She darted away from him and ran between two rows of vines, tears streaming down her face as she saw how some of the grapes were being torn from their bunches to lie on the sodden ground. Half mad with grief, she threw herself down and began to rescue them one by one, her hat soaked and flopping round her face. Rain lashed at her, at the leaves and the fruit.

'Katti, no!' Hugo ordered from behind. He bent and took her arm, forcing her to stand up. 'It's no good. It's pointless. You can't save them all. Save yourself. You're soaked.'

'I don't want your jacket!' she yelled as he tried to put the garment round her. 'You wear it!'

He, too, was wet through, dark hair flat to his head water streaming down a face ravaged by some emotion she was too distraught to interpret.

'Leave me alone, Hugo,' she begged. 'Please leave me alone.'

For a moment he hesitated, watching her with eyes that asked impossible questions. 'You mean that?'

'Yes, I mean it. Just go.'

He turned on his heels and strode away, beginning to run as he reached the grassed linkway. Within seconds he had reached his car. She heard the engine roar into life.

Katarin sank down on her knees and wept, partly for the grapes and partly for the love she could never have. This time, she knew, he would really stay away. And the harvest was ruined.

★ ★ ★

Her grandfather found her some time later, still kneeling in the mud with tears flowing down her face, both hands clutching a few fallen grapes. The downpour had become a steady drizzle, but her world seemed to have ended. Nothing mattered.

'Now come, Katti,' Herr Maier said sternly, rustling up in a rainproof cloak and big hat. 'This will do no good.'

'But they're ruined!' she croaked. 'Look at them, *Opa*.'

'Nah! So we've lost a few. It happens. With

118

vines one has to take what God sends. The bad with the good. Look at you, you're all muddy.'

'Oh, what does it matter?'

He hauled her to her feet, shaking her with a roughness that reached through her misery. 'If you're not concerned about yourself, what of poor old Blitzen standing there in the rain? Take him home and get Gody to give him a good rubdown. And as for you — you take a good hot bath and thank God for all the grapes that are still left. The worst of the storm is done. It's not nearly so bad as I feared. Believe that, Katarin. If you intend to spend your life in wine-growing, then you must learn not to take things so hard. You understand?'

'Yes, *Opa*,' she sighed, wiping rain and tears from her face. 'I'm sorry.'

The pony stood shivering, his flanks twitching while water dripped off his rough brown coat. Murmuring apologies, Katarin stroked his neck, rubbed his ear, and climbed wearily up to the driver's seat.

Along the lanes many cars were parked, the broad slopes of the vineyards dotted with men who had come to survey the storm damage. Ironically enough, the clouds were now flying apart, leaving widening gaps of blue sky. A final flurry of rain came as

119

Katarin turned the trap into the courtyard.

'*Ach, du lieber Gott!*' Frau Gainau exclaimed as Katarin appeared at the door. 'What have you been doing, child? Look at you.'

'Yes, I know,' She glanced down at her soaked, mud-smeared clothes, shuddering. 'I got caught in the rain.'

Catching hold of her, the housekeeper began to hustle her toward the stairs. 'I know all about that. Baron Hugo said he left you up at the Maierstufe. What were you thinking of? You should have let him bring you home.'

'Baron Hugo?' Katarin repeated faintly. 'He was here?'

'He came to fetch your grandfather. He said you were distraught because of the storm. Here, don't trail that mud up the stairs. Take off your jeans here. It's all right, we're alone in the house. I wanted the baron to stay, but he wouldn't. He was soaked to the skin himself. He looked like a ghost, almost gray in the face. And he was obviously worried about you. What came over you, to let yourself get into such a state?'

All-too-ready tears filled Katarin's eyes as with numb hands she peeled off her jeans and gave them to the housekeeper.

'Why, what's wrong?' Frau Grainau asked solicitously. 'What is it, my dear? Not the grapes, surely? Oh, come, come, let me run a bath for you. A nice hot bath, with some of that lovely lemon oil. You'll feel better when you're warm and clean again.'

★ ★ ★

She lay in a hot bath feeling emptied of emotion. Her body ached and her eyes stung from weeping, but she felt calmer than she had for weeks, facing the bitter truth she had refused to accept before — she loved Hugo von Drachensberg more than she had known it was possible to love. And he felt something for her, too, though quite what it was she did not know. Thank God the rain had come before she could shame herself irrevocably.

Whatever she felt, whatever Hugo felt, both of them knew that nothing permanent could ever result from it. She was not the type of girl that a man such as Hugo would choose as a wife. No, Franziska Bader-Wehr was more of his class, 'an appropriate match,' as her grandfather had said. He and Katarin might have indulged in a passionate affair, if she had been so inclined, but it could be no more than that. And since an affair was not what she wanted, then she must ignore her longing for Hugo. It would fade with time. Once the *Weinfest* was over and he married Franziska, he would cease to be a presence in her life. Perhaps he would return to the States, as Berd had said he might.

For the first time Katarin began to wonder if she had really done the best thing when she transferred her life to Gundelheim. Wouldn't it have been better to stay in England, to marry David, spending holidays with *Opa*? Then she would never have met Hugo, never known what she had missed.

6

Most of the wine-growers agreed that the storm, although meaning a setback to their hopes, had not been the disaster that Katarin feared. A year of perfect weather was almost unknown. They were accustomed to facing problems. And since the forecast seemed favorable for the next couple of weeks, the harvesting committee decided that the crop-gathering could begin on the third Monday of September — the Monday of wine festival week. Accordingly, all the vineyards were locked to insure no interference during the last period of ripening.

Now the final cleaning preparations got underway in pressing rooms and cellars. Katarin flung herself into an orgy of scrubbing and washing, but unfortunately the work, while being physically taxing, did not fully occupy her mind. She kept thinking about Hugo, longing for him to come. Before the storm his frequent visits had irritated her, but now she missed him. Several times she fancied she heard the Mercedes go past, but though she paused in her work and waited with fast-beating heart, the vehicle never stopped. She berated herself for imagining that he might arrive. Why should he want to see her when she had sent him away? Besides, he had Franziska.

In the fermentation cellar one day, she was sweeping the floor, trying to clean out all the cobwebby corners behind the tanks and the casks with glass heads, which would show how the wine was clearing. Her grandfather came to find her, bringing a letter in his hand.

'Now what are you doing?' he asked, shaking his head. 'Katti, why don't you rest? You're making work for yourself. If you aren't careful, you'll be too tired to cope with next week. The *Fest* begins on Saturday. Had you forgotten?'

'No, I hadn't forgotten,' she replied, leaning wearily on her broom. 'But I can't sit around doing nothing. You're working.'

'Paperwork, that's all. There's always paperwork to be done. You can come and lend a hand with that, if you must do something.' He pulled a wry face, then remembered the letter he held. 'But look at this. What do you think? It's an invitation from Baron Hugo.'

Her heart jolted at the sound of his name, but she kept her face under control. 'An invitation to do what?'

'To join him on a deer hunt. On Thursday.'

'Good heavens,' Katarin said in disbelief. 'Let me see.'

The letter said exactly what he had told her — he was invited to join a hunting party. The baron intended to go after a deer that would provide the haunch of venison that he had promised to Herr Raichle as a contribution to the feast on Saturday. After the hunt the party would dine at the castle. The letter was typed but signed in blue ink with a flourish that typified the man who had written it.

She looked at her grandfather in amazement. 'You? Hunting deer?'

'And why not?' he demanded. 'In my youth I was a fine shot. I still have my health. I'm not quite ancient yet, you know.'

'But will you go?'

'Yes, of course!' His moustache seemed to bristle and his eyes were bright. 'It's an honor. To hunt with Baron Hugo . . . It's a great privilege. Why should you be surprised? The baron and I are good friends.'

'Yes, I'm sure you are, but — ' She broke off, shaking her head. 'Well, I hope you enjoy yourself.'

'I shall,' he said stoutly. 'Indeed I shall. It will be something to talk about for years afterwards.'

He departed, leaving Katarin wondering why Hugo had sent the invitation. She knew that a sort of camaraderie had sprung up between the two men, but it seemed an odd sort of alliance. She had tried to tell herself that Hugo was cultivating her grandfather only as an excuse to get close to her, but perhaps he had other reasons, though what they were she could only guess.

However, her grandfather was not the only burgher to be honored by an invitation from the baron. Later that day Herr Raichle telephoned to boast that he would be going hunting for deer.

'He was put out when I said I was also going with them.' Herr Maier chuckled as he and Katarin played checkers that evening. '*Liebchen*, you're not concentrating. Look — one, two, three and I have a king. Now you have only two pieces left.'

At that moment the doorbell rang. Hugo, Katarin thought, then, don't be an idiot. Her grandfather heaved himself out of his low chair and went through to the kitchen, while she sat with a piece poised in one hand, her ears tuned in hope and dread for the sound of Hugo's voice.

She was relieved, and bitterly disappointed, when the visitor turned out to be Berd, smartly dressed in suit and silk tie with his fair hair combed into unusual neatness.

'Your grandfather's gone down to the cellar for a bottle of wine,' he told her. 'How are you, Katti?'

'Surviving,' she replied. 'You look very smart, Berd. Are you going out somewhere?'

He gave her a reproachful look. 'Yes. Here. I've come to see you.'

'That's nice,' she said, not caring if he heard the insincerity in her voice. 'You'd better sit down, then.'

'Thank you.' Heavily, he inched past the coffee table where the game board was laid out and lowered himself beside her, perched on the edge of the settee. 'You're playing checkers?'

Katarin bit her tongue to prevent a sarcastic retort from escaping. Berd was not to blame for her loneliness and misery. 'I'm getting soundly beaten, as you can see,' she said, and began to clear the pieces away, putting them in a box.

Berd leaned on his knees, twiddling his thumbs. 'You've heard about this hunting trip, I expect. My father met Herr Raichle earlier. Our good *Bürgermeister* was full of himself. He said your grandfather had been invited, too.'

'Yes, that's right.'

'So have we,' Berd said.

Astounded, she fumbled and dropped the box containing the checkers, which scattered across the carpet. Giving her a puzzled look, Berd knelt and began to gather the pieces, helping her replace them in the box.

'He's invited you and your father?' Katarin said incredulously.

'Half the town council has been invited, though not all of them can take the time for hunting in the middle of the week. Still, they're flattered, even Herr Usee, who must be eighty if he's a day. There's no way you could get him scrambling across mountains in pursuit of deer. But if you ask me, this is just our dear baron's latest attempt to soften us up. He's already made quite an impression on the town.'

'Yes, I know.' Hugo's motives remained a mystery to her, but then she had never found him predictable. 'But since everyone suspected him of villainy even before he arrived on the scene, do you blame him for wanting to win them over? Would *you* like to be unpopular with your neighbors just because they hated your father?'

Idly, he tossed a checkers piece in the air and caught it, weighing it in his hand. 'It depends what he really wants, doesn't it? He's been clever so far, but a man who gets too devious may trip himself up in his own coils. I still say he bears watching.'

'You just won't admit that you might have been wrong about him,' Katarin replied. 'He's probably being neighborly. You won't go, I assume?'

He placed the piece into the box, then smiled unpleasantly at her. 'My father won't, but I shall. I love hunting.'

'Berd! That's hypocrisy!'

'I prefer to think of it as a safety precaution. It's time he and I met again. Perhaps if I spend a day in his company I can fathom what he's really up to.'

'And what if he's just being friendly?'

'I very much doubt that it's as uncomplicated as that, Katti. Why should he suddenly be so friendly to people he regards as inferiors? He was bred to believe himself in authority over people like us. He's a member of the elite, the privileged classes. So why has he taken up with your grandfather?'

'He wanted advice about his vineyard.'

Berd shook his head. 'He could have turned to the greatest experts at the university at Freiburg. They'd have been glad to advise him — and from them he'd have learned the very latest techniques and ideas. Your grandfather knows his business, it's true, but he's old-fashioned in his ways. No, there's more to it.'

Trembling, Katarin stood up. 'Why do you always try to cast doubts about Hugo? You're prejudiced against him, Berd.'

'Perhaps so, but I have reason to be. And why don't you like to listen to me when I talk of him? Are you afraid that one day I might convince you?'

Hearing her grandfather come in, she moved away to put the game board and the box of pieces on a shelf, not replying to Berd's question partly because she was afraid that his assumption was correct.

Herr Maier appeared, triumphantly bearing one of his oldest bottles of wine. 'We'll celebrate. It's not every day a man gets invited to hunt deer. Get some glasses out, please, Katti.'

'I'm going, too,' Berd informed him. 'It should be quite a day.'

'You're going?' Herr Maier repeated in surprise. 'But I thought . . . Well, well, that's good news, Berd. Yes, we'll have some fine sport. When I was a young man . . . '

He lapsed into reminiscences and Berd said no more about his suspicions, though every time the baron's name came into the conversation, he watched Katarin closely as if trying to read her thoughts.

Later, when she saw Berd to the door, he remarked that it was a pity no women had been asked to join the hunt; Katarin would have enjoyed it.

'I might have enjoyed the hunt,' she said, 'but I'm not sure I'd like to see the kill. Besides, Hugo obviously doesn't want women dragging along.'

'That's interesting,' Berd said, watching her narrowly.

'What is?'

'The way you keep referring to him by his first name, as if you were on intimate terms.'

Her eyes glinted above a flush she could not control. 'Don't be silly. I hardly know him.'

'If you say so.'

'I do say so! Are you calling me a liar?'

His mouth smiled, but his eyes remained watchful. 'Would I be so ungallant? I believe you, of course, though it seems strange that most of the girls in Gundelheim sigh over him, while you, who know him better than they do, are unaffected. Don't you find him attractive, Katti?'

'Yes, I do,' she said flatly. 'He *is* attractive. But he belongs to someone else, and in case you'd forgotten *I* have a young man.'

'Who is far away,' Berd added.

'At the moment. I expect to see him soon. Either he will come here or I'll go to England, once the harvest is over. And I expect we'll be getting married very soon,' she added recklessly.

This assertion shook him visibly. 'I see. But from the way you've spoken of him lately, I thought — '

'You had no right to think anything!' she interrupted. 'I'm sorry, Berd, but I do wish you'd keep your nose out of my private life. Our being friends doesn't give you the right to pry.'

'Are we friends?' he muttered. 'Sometimes I wonder. Very soon I shall stop trying. I shall find a girl who appreciates me.'

'I wish you would,' Katarin said. 'You might be happier for it.'

Giving her a final bleak look, he stepped out into the night and she closed the door, sighing to herself. She could hardly bring herself to be civil to Berd anymore. He was the most persistent man she had ever met.

His inclusion in the deer hunt troubled her, for she suspected that he intended to cause trouble. Why on earth had Hugo invited him? In the hope of making peace? If so, it was a forlorn hope. Whatever Hugo had done to Berd in the past, the wounds remained. The thought of them both out on the mountain, in the forest, carrying guns, was suddenly an alarming one.

The following morning she had stripped her bed and was laying the quilt over the balcony to air in the sun when Frau Grainau, sounding agitated, called up the stairs, saying she must come quickly.

Katarin ran out of her room in alarm. 'Whatever's wrong?'

'Telephone for you. Oh, hurry. It's the baroness!'

Something awful had happened to Hugo, she thought in the split-second before common sense told her that if such an eventuality occurred, his mother was unlikely to telephone her, of all people. While Frau Grainau hopped from one foot to the other in the doorway, Katarin picked up the phone.

'Ah, Fräulein Jameson,' came the baroness's cultured voice. 'Good morning. How are you?'

'Good morning, *Baronin*,' Katarin replied, casting a wide-eyed glance at the curious housekeeper. 'I'm very well, thank you. How are you?'

'In excellent health, I'm pleased to say. Now, I expect you're wondering why I called. It's about this hunt my son is planning. I was discussing it with Fräulein Bader-Wehr. We really don't see why the men should have all the fun. Not that we propose to go stalking deer ourselves, but we might follow with a picnic lunch and spend the afternoon walking. The Eimsee Valley is very beautiful at this time of year. Have you been there?'

'Oh — no, I don't think so,' Katarin said, bewildered. Was she being invited to go with the ladies?

'But you must see it!' the baroness exclaimed. 'It's part of our estates, of course, and there are always deer in that area. We shall expect you at . . . say, ten o'clock? If you come up to the castle, we can decide how to organize transport from there on. And perhaps you will be good enough to bring Frau Raichle with you. She doesn't drive, it seems. Of course the men will start out earlier, but we shall be more civilized. Oh . . . and do bring an evening dress with you. You'll want to change before dinner in the evening, I daresay. Good-bye for now, Fräulein Jameson. I look forward to seeing you on Thursday.'

Thoughtfully, Katarin put down the phone, trying to sort out the implications of the invitation. Whose idea had it been? Did Hugo know about it? If she had any sense, she would not go, but the baroness had not given her a chance to refuse. Besides, she wanted to see what might happen between Berd and Hugo. And if she was brutally honest with herself, she wanted most of all, quite simply, to see Hugo.

★ ★ ★

Thursday morning dawned misty and gray. Katarin roused herself early to see her grandfather off in his thick jacket and flat cap to meet the other men in the market square, where they had planned to gather before setting off to the Eimsee Valley, deep in the Black Forest.

As an outfit for the day, she settled for a pair of warm jeans tucked into sturdy boots, a sweater, a navy-blue parka, and a knitted woolen hat. It could be cold in the mountains even though the valley slumbered in mild mists. She packed an overnight bag with her only decent evening dress, but all the time she was steeling herself for coming face to face with Hugo. It would be the first time since their traumatic encounter in the Maierstufe, when more than one storm had raged. Meeting him again would not be easy, but in the company of so many other people she felt she could cope. In some ways the day would be a test to prepare her for the *Weinfest*, when she would have to be beside him in view of the whole town.

She drove into Gundelheim to pick up Frau Raichle, the mayor's wife, who appeared draped in a fur coat that made her look like a well-padded bear, with a matching hat set on freshly curled hair.

'We're very honored,' Frau Raichle said excitedly as she crammed herself into the BMW beside Katarin. 'Of course in the old days the barons of Gundelheim often invited town councillors to the *Schloss*, but it hasn't happened for years and years. Baron Heinrich was not a sociable man. Don't you think it's wonderful that Baron Hugo is bringing back the old closeness?'

'Yes, indeed I do,' Katarin replied.

Her passenger cast her a doubtful glance. 'You're dressed very casually, Fräulein Jameson. We *are* guests of the baroness.'

'I dressed for the weather, and for walking. I thought it was a good idea to be comfortable.'

'But even so . . . '

'Oh, I'll let Fräulein Bader-Wehr be the fashion plate,' Katarin said dryly, sure that Franziska would have some devastating outfit with which she couldn't have hoped to compete.

Frau Raichle's eyes grew round in her fat

face. 'Baron Hugo's fiancée. Will she be there?'

'So I believe.'

'How wonderful! I've seen pictures of her in the magazines. She's very beautiful. And not yet twenty. It's good for a woman to marry young, I always think. Marriage is so fulfilling. Young women who prefer to follow a career seem so unfeminine. It's against nature.'

'Possibly so,' said Katarin sweetly, being polite when she was sure that these pointed remarks were aimed directly at her.

The *Bürgermeister*'s wife had a lot more thinly veiled advice to give as they drove up to the castle, so Katarin was glad when at length the car slipped under the ancient gate arches.

In the courtyard servants loaded picnic hampers into a station wagon, while down the steps came the baroness, Franziska, and their other two guests. The councillors' wives had put on their Sunday best, and Franziska looked glamorous in shocking pink, a close-fitting jumpsuit with high-heeled boots and padded jacket to match. Around her neck she had wound a long white scarf whose tassels danced as she moved. She wore her dark hair tied in a knot on top of her head, and the look she gave Katarin was both haughty and disinterested. Clearly she thought Katarin of no account.

Katarin's immediate reaction of sick, jealous gloom lightened when the baroness greeted her pleasantly. Much to Katarin's amusement, Hugo's mother had chosen to wear a belted raincoat that was far from new over slacks thrust into Wellington boots, with a battered felt hat jammed onto her head. She obviously shared Katarin's preference for comfort.

'Franziska and I will go with Hans in the truck, I think,' the baroness decided. 'Will you follow with the other ladies, Fräulein Jameson? You don't mind driving?'

'No, not at all,' Katarin said, though her delegation as chauffeuse brought a sneer to Franziska's lovely face. Still, what did it matter? It was best to be herself. At least no one could accuse her of trying to impress anyone.

They took a winding route into the heart of the Black Forest, past acres of dark pines, until they reached a narrow road with an alarming drop to the right. It wound round the mountainside, climbing steeply in places, so that clouds closed round like mist. Eventually the road began to descend again, snaking out of the cloud cover to enter a little valley where birch trees trembled yellow leaves and rowan berries made a splash of red among the woods that surrounded a small lake.

In a clearing on the hillside stood a large, log-built chalet with a veranda and balconies sheltered by an enormous hipped roof, its shingles silvered with age. Alongside it were parked the cars that the hunting party must have used, and as the baroness's driver pulled up at the foot of wooden steps, a manservant came out to welcome the ladies with the news that the men would return for lunch in an hour.

'We use this house as a hunting lodge now,' the baroness explained as she led her guests up to the broad veranda where chairs and tables were arranged in small groups. 'They do say that one of my late husband's ancestors was confined here out of harm's way with a guardian some time during the nineteenth century. He's supposed to have been mentally unstable, but I'm not sure that isn't just a trumped-up tale.'

The house was built on an open plan, the comfortable lounge dominated by a fireplace where logs made a welcoming blaze. At the baroness's suggestion, the ladies settled in front of the fire with cups of coffee while the three menservants laid food out on the veranda tables. Franziska lounged in

139

an armchair looking bored, while the three burghers' wives surrounded the baroness, all vying for her attention, with Frau Raichle being particularly obsequious.

'Would you like to go for a walk down to the lake?' Katarin asked Franziska, who replied with a look of astonishment.

'Whatever for? It's cold out there, and the ground's wet. You go if you wish. I don't suppose it matters if *you* get muddy.'

Conscious of a mounting tension inside herself, Katarin left the chalet and wandered down the slope through open woodland, over rough grass where brown leaves lay. Soon Hugo would come. She must behave naturally. Other leaves, yellows and reds, drifted from the trees, and a squirrel paused to stare at her bright-eyed before darting away.

Katarin leaned against the trunk of a silver birch looking at the lovely valley. It was totally unspoiled, except for the hunting lodge, but the house blended pleasantly with the scenery. When snow fell it must be a magical place. How marvelous to live with no neighbors but the birds and animals. If only she and Hugo could be here alone together . . .

'Katarin!' Berd's voice brought her out of impossible dreams. He came striding down the wooded slope toward her, looking fit and pleased with himself. 'There you are! Come on, we're starting lunch and I'm starving.'

Strangely reluctant to move, she levered herself away from the tree, looking up through the woods to where she could see the lodge. 'Are you having a good day?' she asked.

'Oh, yes, it's been very exciting, but no luck so far. We'll try the other side of the valley this afternoon. Hurry up, I haven't eaten since six this morning.'

He seemed in such a good humor that she didn't dare ask how he had got on with Hugo. Perhaps the pleasure of hunting with the baron had made him put aside his prejudice.

The rest of the party had already gathered on the veranda to make a start on the food. Katarin saw Herr Raichle, looking very tired, biting into a chicken leg while he held a glass of wine in his other hand. But naturally it was Hugo's tall figure that she sought out with most interest.

He leaned on the balustrade of the veranda, his dark head bent toward Franziska, who stood in her startling pink beside him. Though he appeared to be listening to what his fiancée was saying, his eyes met Katarin's across the animated group and such conflicting emotions filled her that she had to look away. He was dressed as he had been the first time she had seen him, in a green tweed suit with breeches buckled over the tops of knee boots, but today he had added a suede and leather warmer without sleeves, and in its top button-hole he wore a spray of heather. He looked very much at home in those surroundings, among his warmly clad gamekeepers and stalkers, with guns left leaning against the vehicles and — she noticed suddenly — the huge mastiff lying by his feet, chin on paws.

Katarin ate her lunch in company with her grandfather and Berd, neither of whom seemed to notice how quiet she was. Her grandfather seemed to be in his element, looking forward to continuing the day's sport, though Berd's attention kept wandering along the veranda. Puzzled by the look in his eyes, Katarin followed his glance and realized that he was watching not Hugo but Franziska, who had unbuttoned her padded jacket to reveal that her jumpsuit was daringly unzipped, giving an enticing view to any man who cared to look.

Of course the display was for Hugo's benefit, Katarin thought bleakly. She tried not to glance at him, though she was aware of every move he made. Franziska's bell-like laughter pierced her to the soul, teaching her the agony of jealousy. The girl had attached herself to Hugo with the instincts of a limpet, and knowing that she had every right to do so didn't help Katarin one little bit.

Somehow she managed to conceal what she was feeling, and several glasses of wine helped to numb the pain. She could even laugh at Berd's jokes, though when she realized that Hugo was making his way in their direction her fingers tightened round her wine glass, threatening to snap the slender stem.

In the manner of a good host he came round refilling glasses, but when he reached Katarin she refused any more wine. It loosened her tongue too much.

'Don't you like our wine?' Hugo asked, but before she could reply her grandfather laughed and said that she had been raised on wine from the Maierstufe.

Glancing up, Katarin saw Hugo's wry smile. 'I'm forced to agree that our Drachensberg vintages don't bear comparison with yours, Herr Maier. But I'm doing my best to make improvements.' He looked down at Katarin, his smile altering subtly so that her heart jumped in response. 'Our soil's too good, he tells me.'

'Yes, so he said,' she replied.

'The *Herr Baron* will have to acquire other

land,' Berd said in a soft voice that still managed to inject a sour note. 'Like that of Friedrich Luz. That was a good purchase. His patch is poor enough, and very high up. But it grows excellent wine.'

Hugo's smile still curved his mouth, but the warmth had left his eyes. 'Yes, I believe my father knew what he was doing when he told our agent to offer for Herr Luz's land. Excuse me.'

As he moved away, Berd watched him with narrowed eyes. 'His father! So that's his excuse, is it?'

'Berd . . .' Katarin's grandfather put in with a frown. 'We're the baron's guests today. I'd prefer it if you kept your suspicions to yourself. You have no proof that he shares his father's avaricious ways.'

'Haven't I? You can sit there and say that, Herr Maier? Well, some of us are not so easily blinded. He'll bide his time, no doubt. He can afford to, since he's a young man. But by the time his sons are grown their holdings in the valley will have increased, bit by bit. You see if I'm not right.'

'You talk just like your father,' Herr Maier said in disgust. 'Myself, I judge a man by his actions, and from what I've seen Baron Hugo intends only good for the town and the valley.'

'Oh, I agree,' Berd said, slanting a look to where Hugo stood beside the mayor and Franziska. 'What one sees is all beneficence. But what lies behind it, eh?'

Herr Maier stood up, his eyes sparking over his moustache. 'I won't listen to this. You're unjust, Berd. If you wish to make allegations, then make them in his hearing and let him answer for himself.'

As he moved away Berd smiled cynically at Katarin. 'Your grandfather has gone over to the enemy, it seems. And you?'

'I don't consider Baron Hugo to be my enemy,' she countered stiffly.

'No? Then you've changed your opinion radically. I seem to recall that when you first met him you were annoyed that he should question your ability to run the Maierstufe. Do you think he would stand by and let you take over after your grandfather when he feels as he does?'

Before she could reply someone called to Berd to get ready. The men were preparing to resume the hunt, all except Herr Raichle. The portly *Bürgermeister* had apparently had his fill of exercise for the day.

Katarin saw Hugo go down the steps with her grandfather beside him. Behind them Berd paused to say something to Franziska, who froze him with a look, though after he walked away she watched him assessingly, a hand toying with the toggle of her zipper.

The men departed, making for the far side of the valley. Herr Maier and Berd both waved to Katarin, but Hugo didn't even glance behind him. Being discreet, she thought, but all the same she felt dejected, wishing she could make up her mind about his motives. He strode in the center of the group, the mastiff at his heels, his dark hair lifting in the faint breeze that had dispersed most of the mist.

'Now, ladies,' said the baroness, jamming her felt hat back on her head. 'I intend to walk around the lake. Who's coming with me?' She looked along the veranda to find Katarin. 'You, Fräulein Jameson? You're equipped for walking, by the looks of you.'

'Yes, I'd like to come,' Katarin said, leaving her seat.

The others were torn between their desire to accommodate the baroness and an unwillingness to face a hike of roughly two miles in their best clothes and shoes. Franziska shuddered at the very thought of such an outing and, zipping her jumpsuit up to her throat, said she preferred to remain by the fire.

'Then you ladies stay with Fräulein Bader-Wehr,' the baroness decided. 'There are books and games in the lodge, for your amusement. We shan't be too long, I expect. Come, Fräulein Jameson.'

Obeying this imperious command, Katarin found herself walking beside the baroness, who, despite having to lean on a stick, set a fairly crisp pace, following the road until it petered out into a track that circled the lake. They made small talk until they approached the end of the valley, where a clear stream flecked with foam tumbled down over rocks. A plank bridge provided a way over the water, and the baroness crossed it without hesitation, leading on among deepening woods that glowed with autumn colors.

Abruptly, she stopped, turning to give Katarin a considering look. 'Naturally you are aware that my son admires you,' she said with a blunt frankness that astounded Katarin. 'Well, come, Fräulein Jameson, we are both women of the world. You can tell me the truth.'

What truth? Katarin wondered, her face feeling hot as she fumbled for words. 'The *Herr Baron* and I . . . '

'He's attracted to you,' the baroness said flatly. 'Kindly don't deny it. I know my own son well enough by now. A mother senses these things. It's in his voice when he speaks of you — and it's more in the things he does *not* say. I don't know how far it's gone and I don't want to know, but I assume he has intimated it to you. You did know?'

'Yes, *Baronin*,' Katarin replied, feeling like a schoolgirl brought for reprimand to the headmistress.

'H'm. At least you're honest. I wouldn't have believed you if you denied it. You're not a stupid young woman. It might be easier if you were.'

'Easier?' Katarin managed.

'Easier to believe that he'd fallen prey to quite natural desires. Or lusts, if you prefer. Naturally you know that it can be no more than that. He will marry Franziska. This has been understood for a long time.'

Even Katarin's ears were burning under the woolen hat, mainly from anger that the baroness should choose to warn her off in this arrogant manner.

'You just said that I wasn't stupid,' she replied. 'I'm well aware of right and wrong, *Baronin*. You needn't worry. I'll do nothing to upset your son's plans for the future.'

For another few moments the baroness's cool gray gaze bored into her, then suddenly the look softened and a hand touched Katarin's arm. 'Forgive me for speaking to you in this way. I should have known you were not the sort of girl . . . ' She sighed heavily. 'There have been others. Fortune-hunters. Hugo, being a man, cannot see beyond a pretty face. I had the same trouble with his father. Such men are easy prey to unscrupulous women.'

'I think you underestimate your son,' Katarin said quietly. 'He knows where his duty lies.'

'Duty? You mistake me, Fräulein Jameson. He's very fond of Franziska. If I thought otherwise . . . Is that the way he looks at it — as a duty?'

'It's not something we've ever discussed,' Katarin said. 'His feelings for Fräulein Bader-Wehr are not my concern, after all.'

'No,' the baroness agreed, but her expression was thoughtful. 'It's unfortunate that he's taken it into his head to throw himself so deeply into the festival. I would prefer it if he did not see you again. But since that is impossible . . . I want your word, Fräulein Jameson, that you will not offer him any encouragement. So far, I believe that Franziska is unaware of this . . . this unfortunate attachment he seems to have formed. She is jealous, naturally, of every woman he meets, but I don't think she senses any special danger from you. I wish it to remain that way. You would not wish to come between them, I hope?'

Katarin remained silent, her lips pressed together as she turned over the many answers she might have given. A meek capitulation seemed to be the best course, but the baroness's attitude annoyed her. Hugo was, after all, a grown man.

'Well, Fräulein Jameson?' came the autocratic prompting. 'Will you do as I ask?'

'I've already said I won't interfere with his plans,' Katarin replied. 'But he's quite capable of making his own decisions about that. Have you spoken to him about it?'

The baroness's eyes slid away from her, as if she were embarrassed. 'No. Nor would I like him to know that I had spoken to you. If he thought I had tried to influence you — '

'I had already made up my mind,' Katarin assured her.

'And you'll say nothing?'

'I'm not a troublemaker.'

'No.' The baroness bit her lip unhappily. 'I should have taken the time to get to know you before I spoke. I must apologize, Fräulein Jameson. If you think me an interfering old woman, I can only plead a mother's concern. I want only what is best for my family. I . . . I think I shall go back now. The lake is larger than I remembered. But you go on. There's no hurry.'

As the baroness turned away to retrace her steps to the plank bridge, Katarin was convinced that the walk had been an excuse to get her alone, to persuade her to drop any ambitions she might have harbored. Once again she had been firmly put in her place as a person of little account in the von Drachensbergs' plans.

But, perversely, the lecture had only served to make her wonder how Hugo really felt about Franziska. The girl was beautiful, but very young and inclined to sulk, and she had no taste for outdoor pursuits, which Hugo obviously loved.

Disturbed by the trend of her thoughts, she thrust her hands into her coat pockets, hunched her shoulders, and began to walk with her eyes on the passing ground. How many times did she have to go through this argument with herself before she was convinced? Hugo von Drachensberg was not for her. Definitely and absolutely not. But it was a hard thing to accept.

★ ★ ★

After a while, almost without realizing it, she found that she had climbed up to where the soft woods gave way to evergreens. Suddenly a shot sounded, and then another, some distance off. Katarin stopped to listen. She had all but forgotten about the hunt.

A patch of thicker mist moved up to enclose her. Through it the trees loomed dark and mysterious, and there came a sound she could not at first identify — a soft thudding. A roe deer appeared like a ghost through the mist, balked at the sight of her and changed direction, charging off down the slope, followed by a stream of others.

And then she heard the mastiff baying in pursuit of the deer. It came bounding out of the cloud and stopped, its great head lifted, fangs bared, barking in a deep, throaty voice that reverberated among the trees. Half-afraid, Katarin backed up, her eyes fixed on the dog as a piercing whistle sounded behind it.

'Lint!' a male voice called sharply, and Hugo's tall figure detached itself from the mist.

As soon as she had heard the shot, seen the deer and the dog, this meeting had seemed inevitable, but if she had half-expected it Hugo had not. He stopped in his tracks, staring at her in amazement, saying, 'Katarin?'

152

'I . . . I was out for a walk,' she faltered. 'I didn't realize you were in this area — not until I heard the shots. Have you . . . have you been successful?'

'A fine buck,' he said, his eyes fixed on her face asking silent questions. 'Lindwurm ran off. I shall have to train him better!'

Her mind veered in several directions at once. Did he think she had deliberately tracked him down? Where were the other men? And after her conversation with the baroness what was she supposed to say to Hugo?

Grasping for some safe subject, she glanced at the now-silent dog. 'Lindwurm? That's another way of saying 'dragon,' isn't it?'

'Yes.' He gave her a small, wry smile. 'It's a private joke — a play on words. I'm of the family from Dragon Mountain, from Dragon Castle . . . '

'That's what I thought,' she said, pain twisting inside her as she returned the smile. 'Well . . . the others will wonder where you are. You'd better rejoin them now you've found the dog.'

A corner of his mouth lifted ruefully and his eyes looked grayer than ever. Gray as the mist. Gray with sorrow. 'Before I forget myself again, you mean? . . . Are you alone?'

'I came out walking. I had no idea you were anywhere around or I wouldn't . . . ' The sentence trailed off as the expression in his eyes penetrated the defences she had raised.

'You don't have to explain,' he said quietly. 'We understand each other very well, you and I. But I'm glad of this chance to talk with you. We still have the *Weinfest* to get through.'

'I hadn't forgotten. But it shouldn't be too difficult to cope with it. If we behave like sensible adults — '

He cut her off with a laugh that sounded full of pain. 'The two don't always go together. To be adult is not necessarily to be sensible, as I've been demonstrating these past few weeks. I've been behaving like a schoolboy. Forgive me for that, Katarin.'

'I . . . ' Tears boiled in her throat, choking her. 'I was to blame, too. But it's over, Hugo.'

'I know that,' he said quietly. 'When the *Weinfest* is done I'll never trouble you again, but I would like to think we can remain friends.'

Taking the heather from his buttonhole, he walked slowly toward her, holding out the spray between finger and thumb. Silently Katarin accepted the offering, looking down at the stiff branchlets and tiny purple flowers.

Hugo stood a bare two feet away, his vitality reaching out to encompass her. She sensed that he was poised between discreet withdrawal and some action that would ignite the fires that smoldered between them. Tension held her immobile, her head bent, wanting him to touch her and yet praying that he would not, while tears bloomed hot against her lashes.

They both stiffened and looked up the hill as a stick cracked. The dog gave a soft 'Woof,' peering into the mist, but a word from Hugo made him relax.

'Someone spying?' Katarin breathed, and without thinking laid a hand on the tweed of his sleeve. 'Oh, Hugo . . . '

'And if we were seen, what can he make of it?' he asked, scanning her face with hunger. A gentle finger wiped a tear from her cheek, tipped up her chin, and he bent to press his lips to a corner of her mouth with infinite tenderness. As she blinked up at him through her tears, a shudder of longing ran through her.

The dog barked again, and this time there came a scuffling as of someone slipping on the carpet of needles. Hugo glanced round, his mouth tightening. He swore and said, 'Go back to the lodge, Katti,' and began to climb in pursuit of the unknown watcher. A snap of his fingers took the huge dog bounding after him.

For a moment Katarin stood watching the place where he had disappeared into the mist, then she gently put the heather in her pocket and started back down the hill.

7

Katarin reached the lodge to find the ladies and Herr Raichle waiting to depart. They had heard the shots and guessed that the men would soon appear with their trophy, but since the clouds were closing down it was decided that the women should return to the castle at once before the weather made the roads too dangerous. As they climbed into their two cars, however, the first of the hunting party trekked up. Katarin saw her grandfather, looking pleased with himself, but there was no sign of Hugo — or of Berd.

At the castle she waited on tenterhooks for the men to join the party. When at last the main door opened and the hunting party strode in, all talking animatedly, she was relieved to see Hugo laughing with her grandfather, while Berd came behind in conversation with another man. All appeared to be normal, and only the briefest of glances between her and Hugo reminded her of that fraught scene in the Eimsee Valley.

She was very much aware of the baroness watching her, and of Franziska sinuously walking to join Hugo as more coffee was served.

'It's been a good day!' her grandfather said, flopping onto a settee beside her. 'I shall sleep tonight.'

'Yes, I'm tired, too,' Katarin said. '*Opa* . . . would you mind very much if we didn't stay to dinner? I've got the most awful headache.' It was not a lie. During the drive home a niggling pain in her temple had become a raging ache that numbed her entire brain.

Her grandfather studied her pale face for a moment, then patted her knee. 'Of course, *Liebchen*. Let's go and take our leave of the baroness.'

Murmuring words of sympathy, the Baroness Anna shook Katarin's hand in farewell, but from the look in her eyes she knew well enough that Katarin was leaving partly because of their earlier discussion. The party shifted and muttered as it became apparent that Herr Maier was giving up his chance to have dinner at the castle. Slowly, inexorably, her grandfather led her to where Hugo was standing, to make formal goodbyes.

She said, '*Auf Wiedersehen*' to Franziska, whose hand felt as cold and limp as a dead fish; then she risked a glance at Hugo's face and found him regarding her with concern as his warm hand closed round hers.

'I hope you'll soon feel better,' he said. 'You'll need to be well for Saturday.'

Katarin could never remember whether she replied in words or whether they communicated by look and touch of hands, but she left the castle knowing that Hugo was concerned for her, and sad. Life was so unfair, she thought. If he hadn't been who he was . . . If Franziska hadn't existed . . . But such wishful thinking was useless. She must accept that loving Hugo was a dead-end lane.

★ ★ ★

They returned home to find that a parcel had arrived bearing a hand-written message, 'Costumes for the Wine Queen.' Katarin stared at it in despair.

'Aren't you going to open it?' her grandfather asked.

'No, not now.' She tossed the parcel onto a couch in the window alcove and opened the refrigerator. 'I'll get us something to eat, and then I think I'll go to bed.'

Her grandfather watched her thoughtfully. 'Are you going to tell me about it, Katti?'

'About what?' she asked.

'Oh, nothing, nothing,' he said with a shrug.

'There's nothing to tell, *Opa*. Honestly.'

'If you say so,' he replied, though his expression told her he knew she was lying.

She turned away, occupying herself with preparing a meal while he poured himself a glass of *Schnaps* and sat down to read the newspaper. The presence of the parcel tormented her curiosity, however, and she kept glancing at it, wanting to see the costumes but hating to face the thought of what they meant — pure agony for the coming week.

'Well, open it, *Liebchen*,' her grandfather said eventually. 'Suppose they don't fit? Come on — I want to see them even if you don't.'

Half-reluctantly she untied the string that bound the parcel, catching her breath as the glitter of gold-colored braid on wine-red velvet was revealed. It was a full-length cloak, edged with braid and tied with gold tasseled cords.

'Wonderful!' Herr Maier exclaimed. 'What else? A gown?'

'Yes. Oh . . . look, *Opa*!' She lifted out the garment, which was made of colors echoing the green of the vine and the yellow of ripe grapes, cut in floating panels over a full underdress that would fit most figures. With it came a belt of gold cord to match the fastening on the cloak.

Katarin held it against her body, trying to see how it would look, enchanted despite her headache and her fears.

A newly gilded crown of vine leaves lay on top of the final item in the parcel, an evening gown. With shaking hands she took it out and held it up, staring at the pure whiteness of layered chiffon.

'Is that for the grand ball?' her grandfather inquired. 'You'll look like — '

'Like a bride,' she finished for him, a catch in her throat. 'That's the way I'm meant to look, isn't it? It's beautiful, don't you think?'

'Gundelheim has never seen such a Wine Queen as you will make,' he said somberly, adding without change of tone, 'Why didn't you tell me you had decided to marry David?'

'What?' she stared at him blankly, the ball gown draped softly across her arm. 'Whatever gave you that idea?'

'Isn't it true?' he asked, frowning. 'Berd said you had told him you had definitely decided — '

'*Opa*! I only said that to stop him from asking questions. I haven't decided anything, except that I must talk to David. In person.'

'He won't come here to live,' he said with a shake of his head.

'We don't know that for sure. That's why I must see him. We must get things settled, one way or another.'

'What if he asks you to go back to England? If that's what you want, you must do it. Don't worry about me. I lived alone before you came. I can manage alone again. But you know I've always dreamed of leaving you the Maierstufe. It has been in our family for two hundred years. I'd like to think of its remaining in the family. If it has to be sold . . .'

Though she was upset and confused, the answer came to her with instinctive clarity. 'It won't. I promise you that. I'll look after it, and my children after me.'

'David's children?'

She hesitated, still unable to decide. Her heart might cry for the moon but her head spoke more sensibly. 'I'm really not sure, *Opa*. That's why I want to see him again. Face to face I should be able to tell how he really feels. Maybe I can finally decide what *I* feel. But until I see him . . . I just don't know.'

* * *

After a restless night she slept late the next morning, finally tempted out of her bed by the bright sunlight across her window. Autumn yellows tinted the trees in the valley, but the sky was blue and the air warm. Indian summer, hoped for by everyone involved in wine-growing, had arrived in Gundelheim.

In a vase on her dressing table the spray of heather reminded her of Hugo as she showered and dressed. She would keep it forever, she thought, as she tenderly touched the stiff branchlets. At least she would have one secret memento of him.

Whether because of the sunlight, the lovely costumes she had to wear, or a fatalistic acceptance of realities, she made up her mind to enjoy the *Weinfest*. For a whole week she could be in Hugo's company openly, without anyone thinking anything of it, and if she stole a few hours' pleasure from it, then who was to know? There would be time for remorse when it was all over.

★ ★ ★

The next day she woke early to face the prospect of the opening ceremony of the wine festival, and somehow the endless morning passed.

After lunch, while Frau Grainau rushed here and there chivying her into haste,

163

Katarin put on the gown of green and yellow panels, fastening the gold cord round her slender waist, then donned the velvet cloak. It felt beautiful to the touch, almost like fur, as it swirled around her. Against its deep redness her hair lay in soft curls, the color of apricots, as Hugo had once described it.

'Put on your crown,' Frau Grainau commanded. 'Oh — that's wonderful. Wonderful! You really look like a queen. I can't wait to see what Baron Hugo will be wearing. Hurry, now, hurry! The parade's due to start at two-thirty. You don't want to be late.'

Her grandfather was equally complimentary, and as he drove her through the back streets, several people stared at the sight of her crowned and cloaked in velvet. It seemed that hundreds of people had gathered by the little railway station, where the parade was to start, and Herr Maier was obliged to park some distance away. So Katarin made her first public appearance to a crush of people, who all smiled and exclaimed in delight over her costume as they cleared a way for her.

Ahead, through the crowd, she glimpsed the flower-covered structure on which she must ride. The place milled with people in traditional dress, girls in white with real vine leaves in their hair, and bandsmen in braided uniforms. Then suddenly the throng parted and she saw Hugo, tall and imposing in a velvet cloak the exact frosted blue of 'black' grapes, worn over a flowing burgundy-color robe. On his dark head a crown similar to her own gleamed, worn straight across his brow. As he caught sight of her he hesitated, then strode swiftly toward her, the robe swirling round long legs, the braided cloak flowing behind. He looked devastating, like some barbarian lord of the Middle Ages who might easily throw her across his saddlebow and ride off. The look in his eyes made her wonder if he had had the same thought himself, for there was in his face no trace of the sorrow he had shown at their last meeting.

Taking her hand, he made a bow to which she replied with a deep curtsy. The crowd laughed and applauded, obviously thrilled by the new costumes, but Hugo's smile had an air of recklessness about it that made Katarin catch her breath as she allowed him to lead her toward their conveyance. A vineyard cart had been transformed into a fairy carriage by means of thousands of flowers, with petal-decked chairs set beneath a vine-twined arch lush with bunches of real grapes. The cart was drawn by two oxen, whose horns had also been adorned with vines, and the driver wore a brown tunic with an ancient drinking horn slung round his shoulders.

Another traditional feature of the *Weinfest* was the Knight of the Vine, who played court jester with the crowds. He wore armor constructed of papier-mâché and silver foil, but beneath the raised visor of his helmet was the face of Hans Leitner, a burly butcher.

Under cover of the flurry of activity around them, his hand found hers, holding it possessively tight, though he didn't glance down at her. She replied with pressure of her own and it was enough.

'Right!' someone called. 'Take your places, everyone.'

Without hesitation Hugo turned and took Katarin by the waist, lifting her into the cart, where she sat in the left-hand seat as he climbed up beside her, giving her a look of naked longing.

'You look beautiful,' he said in a tense undertone, using English. 'I want to kiss you.'

She stared at him wide-eyed, startled and shocked. 'Well, don't.'

'No.' With a grimace he seated himself on his 'throne.' 'Not here, anyway.'

'Hugo!' she croaked. 'You wouldn't — '

'No, of course I wouldn't. Let's go

on pretending.' He turned on a smile, acknowledging a shout from somewhere in the crowd, and the moment had gone, though Katarin could not forget it. His mood seemed so different from the last time she had seen him that she wondered what could have happened.

Ahead of them the bands and dancers sorted themselves out into lines, ribbons fluttering and instruments gleaming in the sun. On either side of the cart the Queen's 'maidens,' dressed in white, held colored streamers. At the rear came the Knight of the Vine; riding a patient horse that would not object when he began rolling as if inebriated, waving a bottle of wine from which he took frequent sips. The bottle was empty, in fact; Hans Leitner would need all his wits to play the part of buffoon — to begin with, anyway.

The band struck up, the glockenspiel's bright tinkle sounding above the blare of brass and the beat of the drum. Everyone cheered as the parade began to move, the flowered cart rumbling into life behind the plodding oxen. The young girls waved their streamers and Katarin found herself waving her hand at the crowds filled with tourists and townspeople alike who lined the route.

Beside her Hugo played his part with

amiable dignity, while to Katarin the whole thing took on the aspect of some insane dream. She waved and smiled, smiled and waved, all the time wondering how she ever came to be riding in a shaking, swaying oxcart beside Hugo von Drachensberg.

Eventually the parade entered the square, where spectators craned for a good view of the ceremonies. At the far side of the marketplace, not far from the linden tree, two fires blazed with spits set over them to support the roasting ox and venison, with men standing by to turn the meat and keep it basted. By evening, when the feast began, the meat would be ready to slice and sell, raising funds for charity.

Little booths stood ready for the selling of wines from all the different vineyards, and on a stand a vast barrel waited to be broached. Beside it lay the flower-decked dais from where the King and Queen would preside over the festivities.

The cart rattled over a stretch of cobbles, giving its occupants an uncomfortable ride before it stopped by the dais. With a swirl of his cloak Hugo leaped down, turning to hold out his arms to Katarin, a rueful smile on his face.

'I should have asked them to put better springs on our carriage,' he said. 'I was starting to feel seasick.'

She leaned down, placing her hands on his shoulders as he swept her from the cart to stand beside him, and for a second his hands lingered caressingly on her waist as he smiled down at her. Then the band played a fanfare and the Wine King escorted his Queen to their thrones on the dais, while her young attendants ranged themselves on either side and the Knight of the Vine performed a tipsy dismount that had the crowd laughing.

Another blare of trumpets announced the arrival of Herr Raichle, emerging from the Town Hall resplendent in his *Bürgermeister*'s robes and chain of office with his councillors around him. He made a brief speech requesting that the King should announce the start of the *Fest,* and with a fine flourish Hugo stood up and declared the celebrations open.

That was Katarin's cue to accept with queenly grace a horn of wine drawn from the great cask. With a curtsy, she presented it to Hugo, who said in an undertone, 'I wish you were always so subservient, my lady,' and gave her a wickedly twinkling look before drinking from the horn, returning it to her.

The wine proved rather bitter, one of the less noble vintages, but it served to quench her dry throat. She handed it next to the Knight of the Vine, who managed to overbalance as he attempted to bow to her, causing a fresh wave of laughter before he drained the horn to applause from the crowd.

Katarin resumed her seat, relieved that the first formalities were over. The band struck up a lively tune and the crowd surged forward, gathering round the wine booths to sample the wares. An attendant brought glasses of wine to the dais and there was time to relax while the square swirled with activity and music. Hans Leitner, in his ungainly armor, moved among the throng wreaking mayhem, bringing shrieks of laughter.

Feeling uncertain of the strange mood Hugo appeared to be in, Katarin was glad that Herr Raichle and some of the councillors remained on the dais chatting.

'Ah, well,' Herr Raichle said eventually. 'We must circulate, if you'll excuse us. There are many visitors in Gundelheim today and one must give a good impression.'

As the town councillors drifted away to their civic duties, Hugo stood up, shaking out his cloak, looking down at Katarin with veiled eyes. 'We must mingle, too. I'd prefer to keep you to myself, but convention makes demands.'

Again he spoke in English, in case anyone

should overhear, and she replied in the same language, feeling flustered. 'I wish you wouldn't . . . You're not making it very easy for either of us.'

'Who said things had to be easy?' he demanded.

Wondering what devil had got into him, she rose to her feet, smoothing down her paneled gown. To her dismay Hugo stepped closer and adjusted the set of her cloak, and her crown, his fingers caressing her hair and shoulders.

'Hugo!' she protested in a whisper.

His eyebrow quirked sardonically. 'You must look tidy, my lady. Come.' Offering her his hand, he stepped down from the dais, his eyes fixed on her face in a way that brought color rushing to her cheeks. She glanced away, and to her discomfort she met the cynical gaze of Berd Langren, watching from beside the big wine-cask, where girls in traditional dress dispensed glasses of wine for a nominal sum. Berd lifted a glass in a mocking toast and drained it in one gulp, so that a shiver of disquiet ran through Katarin.

'Are you cold?' Hugo inquired.

'No.'

'You shivered,' he informed her.

Convulsively her hand tightened round his.

'Someone walked over my grave, that's all. Hugo . . . did you find out who it was on the mountainside the other day?'

'Not exactly. Not to say for sure. Why?'

'Was it Berd?'

Again he tilted that eyebrow at her, surveying her face with a mixture of amusement and tenderness. 'It might have been. Does it matter? Whoever it was, it was too misty for him to have seen much. What were we doing, after all?'

'We were being indiscreet. It must stop, Hugo. You promised — ' She gasped as his fingers threatened to crush hers and his expression changed to one of audacious challenge.

'During the *Fest* the Wine King reigns supreme. He is lord of all — and that includes his Queen. I may decide to throw discretion to the winds, and then what will you do about it, Katarin?'

She stared at him in horror, hardly believing her ears. 'You can't be serious.'

'I was never more serious in my life,' he told her in a low, vibrant voice. 'And kindly take that look off your face, Miss Jameson. You're supposed to be happy. You're Queen of the festival.'

He swept her away, and they spent the remainder of the afternoon mixing with the crowds, exchanging banter with residents and answering questions from visitors, many of whom had come from other parts of Germany, or from abroad. Katarin managed to live up to her role, though she was disturbed by the way Hugo kept touching her at every opportunity, either holding her hand or sometimes laying his arm across her shoulders. Beneath her apparent gaiety she was terrified that someone might notice, but as she drank several more glasses of wine, she, too, lost her sense of propriety and began to wonder whether it mattered what people thought. At festival time everyone went a little mad.

Toward the end of the afternoon, when her legs were aching and her head beginning to swim, Katarin saw her grandfather approaching through the noisy crowd.

'It's time we went home,' he said. 'You're starting to look tired, *Liebchen*. You'll have no energy for tonight unless you rest.'

'I was thinking the same,' Hugo agreed.

'Then let's go. I've brought the car as near as I could. It's just up here.'

Herr Maier led the way, and Katarin found no point in questioning the fact that Hugo came with them, his arm lightly round her waist as they left the merry people in the square, few of whom noticed their departure.

It was a relief to flop into the BMW for the short drive to her grandfather's house, and then to relax in the quiet sitting room while Frau Grainau brought coffee and food. Katarin was almost too tired to think or take note of what was happening.

After a while she excused herself and went up to her room to change out of her costume. Wrapped in a loose dressing gown, she lay on her bed to rest and drifted into sleep.

She woke from jumbled dreams to feel a draft blowing on her face. A draft? she thought sleepily, not opening her eyes. From where?

It came again — a warm breath that stirred the tendrils of hair round her ear — and with a start she realized it had human origins. Her eyes snapped open and she looked dazedly into Hugo's smiling face, very near her own. Around him, the room was full of shadows as the daylight faded.

'You look lovely when you're sleeping,' he murmured.

Realizing that he was actually in her bedroom, kneeling by her bed, Katarin sat up in horror, pulling the dressing gown securely round her. 'What are you doing here?'

He sat back on his heels, a curious gleam in gray eyes beneath the tumble of dark hair.

He, too, had discarded his costume to reveal the shirt and slacks he had worn beneath. The shirt was open at the neck, the sleeves rolled up to display brown forearms. 'I was sent to wake you,' he said. 'Your grandfather has a visitor and Frau Grainau has gone home, so someone had to remind the Wine Queen of her duties. We have half an hour before we're due to attend the feast.'

'Half an hour?' A glance at her watch confirmed that he was right. 'Oh, heavens, why did you let me sleep so long? I shouldn't have had so much wine.'

'You needed the rest. Tonight we must dance in the square. I've never danced with you, Katarin. I'll enjoy it. Will you?'

She stared at him in despair. 'You know I will. But, please, Hugo, you shouldn't be in my room. What will my grandfather think?'

'He won't know. He's gone down to his cellars with the man who came. We're alone in the house.'

As he started to rise and reach for her, Katarin scrambled away, gaining the comparative safety of the other side of the bed. She was alarmed by the odd, reckless mood he had been in all day, for it could mean scandal for both of them.

'What's got into you?' she gasped as he softly came round the bed, tall and lithe, with a determined light in his eyes that made her back away until she found herself cornered, her hands held out to fend him off. 'Please don't!' she begged frantically. 'Don't spoil everything.'

He crooked a wicked eyebrow, continuing to approach until he met the barrier of her hands. 'I only want to kiss you,' he said under his breath. 'Either you allow me or I steal it by force. Robber baron, remember?'

'You're not being fair,' she groaned, vividly aware of his warmth through the thin shirt. It seemed to spread from her fingertips to invade all her senses, making her arms feel weak, so when he reached out her elbows bent to allow him close enough to lace his hands behind her, drawing her slowly nearer. In the twilight of the room his eyes seemed to glow with inner light, mesmerizing her until nearness drove his face out of focus and with a sigh she closed her eyes, lifting her lips to his.

It was all wrong, she thought despairingly, but her senses rejoiced in the feel of his firm, warm flesh as she wrapped her arms round his neck and felt herself drawn to lean against him like a pliant willow, her body curved to his. Everything in her strained toward him, wanting to possess and encompass him if only for this moment.

'You're so soft,' he murmured. 'You smell so good.' He bent his head to lay gentle kisses down her throat, and she let her fingers play in his hair, giving herself up to the pleasure of his caresses as his lips moved down to the soft swell of flesh where her robe had parted.

'I want your word!' The baroness's voice rang in Katarin's head and suddenly it was as if Hugo's mother had materialized in the room, watching with reproach and anger.

'Don't!' Katarin breathed, her hands in his hair making him lift his head to look at her with burning eyes.

'Why not?' he asked raggedly.

'You know why not!'

He pulled her close again, pressing her to the length of his body as he looked down into her face. 'I know that your voice says one thing when your eyes say another. If I choose to believe your eyes, who can blame me?'

'I can,' she managed, struggling for sanity to deny the coursing of blood that ran through her veins like hot wine. 'I've asked you . . . I keep asking you . . . Why are you doing this, Hugo? Does it feed your ego to know I can't hold out against you?'

A shadow seemed to cross his eyes in the instant before he released her and stepped away, then the challenging light was back.

'Before this week is out I'll make you agree with your eyes. I'm Wine King.'

'You're drunk,' she said flatly.

At this he laughed aloud. 'Maybe so. But not from wine. Now come, *Liebling*, get ready. We mustn't be late.'

'And don't call me . . . ' she began, but he had whirled away and was gone, still laughing, leaving her more disturbed than ever.

She sank down onto her bed, head in hands, waiting for the clamor of her blood to subside and let her breathe more easily. How very easy it would have been to make love with him. He was so strong, so desirable. Shocked at her own thoughts, she shook herself, dismissing her physical need of him.

She did not understand him. Only two days ago he had asked her forgiveness for the way he had behaved. He had virtually said that he would not tempt her further. So why was he now willing to throw caution aside so blatantly?

★ ★ ★

She continued to wonder about it as she sat on the dais in the market square that evening. The place blazed with light, colored bulbs strung along shop fronts and in the trees;

178

the Town Hall was floodlit and roasting fires blazed bright as the meat sent out a mouth-watering scent. A small merry-go-round spun dazzlingly, giving rides to children, its music vying with the sound of pipers who played for a lively exhibition of folk dancing, while long tables had been set up with benches on either side where people swayed to the music.

A sense of unreality held Katarin in thrall as she watched the dancers whirl and slap their legs. They were dressed in traditional folk costumes, the men in leather shorts and braided jackets, the women arrayed in embroidered aprons over full-skirted dresses worn with shawls and tall hats aflutter with ribbons and encrusted with beads. Around them those who could not find seats stood to watch, while others moved about on the periphery, buying wine or gathering to share in the feast as the great roasts were sliced.

Beside her, Hugo seemed amused by everything. He constantly drew her attention to incidents among the crowd — the Knight clowning, two boys engaged in a tussle, someone wearing a ferocious wooden mask, someone else reeling drunkenly. Not for a moment did he allow her to forget his presence in the spangled night, though she was relieved to note that he drank sparingly of the wine with which he was plied. For herself, she only took a sip now and then, knowing she must keep a clear head. Beneath the merriment that surrounded her, her nerves thrummed like an overstrung violin for fear that Hugo might do something outrageous. And from the gleam in his eye she guessed that he was well aware of her fears.

Children from the schools sang and danced in the square, their young voices sweet against the oompahs from the band, and when they had taken their applause it was time for general dancing, which traditionally was begun by the Wine King and his 'betrothed.'

Rising majestically to his feet, Hugo bowed low before her, offering her his hand, and Katarin allowed herself to be led to the center of the cleared space. Light flickered across the laughing faces of their audience as he took her in his arms and whirled her into a polka more energetic then elegant. The crowd surged forward, swirling round them as everyone joined in, glad of the exercise in the cool night air.

When at last the music stopped she was breathless, disoriented by the whirling of the dance, and she had no strength to protest as Hugo looped his arms around her and let her lean on him. She could feel his heart thudding from the exertion as he brushed his cheek against her temple and laughed down at her, resuming a dance hold as the band swung into a waltz.

Eventually she found herself dancing with Berd, who had appeared from nowhere to lay hold of her and drag her into the melee. He had been drinking heavily. His face was red, his eyes bright with mischief and malice, and he held her much too tightly, laughing when she objected. Finally he dragged her into the shadows beneath the linden tree and tried to kiss her, fastening his arms round her waist when she tried to get away.

'Berd, stop it!' she gasped. 'You're making a spectacle of yourself.'

'No one's looking,' he said hoarsely. 'Besides, they're all too drunk to care.'

His mouth swooped again and she turned her head aside, pushing at him with all her might.

'Oh, come on, Katti,' he muttered, 'Franziska Bader-Wehr didn't fight me. She enjoyed kissing me.'

She became still, staring at him in light-speckled darkness as a chill of disquiet caught at her heart. 'You don't expect me to believe that, I hope?'

'I don't care whether you believe it or not. It's true. She was bored to tears in all that stuffy company last Thursday evening, and your Baron Hugo was too busy playing host to those stupid, gullible people fawning round him. So Franziska and I found ourselves a nice quiet corner in the library. We were getting pretty friendly until he walked in on us.'

'He?' she breathed. 'Who?'

'Your Baron Hugo, of course. And he was livid. But I don't care. For once I got the better of him. I took something that was his, instead of the other way around.'

'Berd, is this true?' she asked, her head swimming with all the implications of this news. It would explain so much.

'Do you think I'd make it up?' he demanded. 'Why shouldn't she have a little fun with me when he's busy chasing *you* for all the world to see? Are you cold with him, Katti? Are you?'

His arms tightened round her waist, threatening to stop her breath, and she saw the gleam of bared teeth before she twisted her head away, straining to free herself.

'He doesn't fool me anymore,' he grated. 'It's not you he wants, it's the Maierstufe. Why else has he been flattering your grandfather? Why else should he pay so much attention to you? He's after the vineyard, one way or another. I always told you not to trust him.'

'I suggest,' a cold voice said from close beside them, 'that you let the young lady go, Herr Langren.' Hugo stood there, simmering with a fury that Katarin sensed strongly even though his face was half-concealed by shadow. In the long cloak with the vine crown set across his brow he looked formidable.

Released from Berd's brutal grasp, she leaned against the tree, watching Berd straighten himself with the dignity of the inebriate. He faced Hugo's frown with unflinching disdain, shrugging as if he didn't care, then without a word he turned and walked away, heading unsteadily for the nearest wine booth.

'Are you all right?' Hugo asked. 'He didn't hurt you?'

'No,' she got out. 'No, I'm fine.'

'You don't sound fine,' he said, moving closer. 'Katarin — '

'Don't touch me! Don't . . . ' Too confused to think, she brushed past him and ran through the crowd to the side street that would take her home. If anyone wondered why the Wine Queen had departed in such a hurry, she didn't care. She couldn't have borne to be near Hugo a moment longer.

8

Reaching the sanctuary of home, she fled to her room and tore off her Wine Queen's costume. Wine Queen! That was a laugh. She went to the bathroom and stood beneath the shower, letting it run as hot as she could stand over her hair and down her body as she soaped away the memory of the day, especially those moments in the bedroom when she had allowed Hugo an intimacy she now regretted. She had believed, poor fool, that he cared about her, but now she understood the wild, daredevil mood he had been in all day, and she told herself she hated him. Certainly she hated herself for being taken in by him.

Eventually, wrapped in a bath towel with another towel round her hair, she emerged from the steam-filled bathroom to find her grandfather waiting by the head of the stairs. He looked worried, for which she was sorry.

'I just suddenly felt very tired,' she said with a sigh. 'I'm sorry, *Opa*. I thought I'd come quietly home and not bother you when you were enjoying yourself. You needn't have left the *Fest*.'

'I'd had enough, anyway,' he replied. 'But you needn't lie to me, *Liebchen*. Baron Hugo told me what happened.'

Her lips compressed bitterly. 'Oh, did he?'

'Yes. He said Berd upset you. But, child, you know what Berd is like. He wanted to be Wine King. It's been eating at him all these weeks. And he'd had too much to drink. You shouldn't let him bother you.'

'It's not just Berd. Oh, why did Hugo have to come running to you? Why doesn't he mind his own business?'

'He was concerned for you!' her grandfather exclaimed, his brow knotting as if he didn't understand her. 'What else should he have done?'

'He might have just left me alone for once!' she cried. Striding into her room, she sat down in front of the mirror and began to towel her hair vigorously while her grandfather stood in the doorway reasoning with her.

'This isn't like you, Katti. You must be over-tired. Baron Hugo was most upset about what happened.'

'Yes, I'll bet he was!' she retorted, and draped the damp towel round her neck, her hair in a tangle as she turned to him. '*Opa* . . . hasn't it ever occurred to you how odd it is that he's started coming to you for advice about everything?'

'Odd?' he repeated with a frown. 'In what way?'

'I mean . . . why did he choose you?'

He spread his hands in bewilderment. 'Why not me? I have as much experience in wine-growing as any man in Gundelheim. And we get along very well, the baron and I.'

'I know that. But do you realize that he once told me I'd never be able to run the Maierstufe?'

'Oh, that's nonsense. Nonsense!'

'Is it? Even Berd said the Association had their doubts about accepting me. Have they . . . have they said anything to you?'

'One or two hints have been dropped,' he admitted. 'But I shall leave my property as I choose, not how they dictate. The Maierstufe will be yours, whatever they say, and if you wish to run it yourself, then you shall do so. But when that day comes they will be used to the idea.'

'I ought to have been a boy,' Katarin said glumly, chin on hands as she stared at her tousled reflection. 'Then nobody would have given it a second thought.'

Through the mirror she saw her grandfather watching her in silent reproach. 'You think

I'm an old fool, letting Baron Hugo make use of me? You think he could persuade me to sell the Maierstufe?'

'No, of course not. It's just . . . I don't understand him. I've got a feeling it must have something to do with the vineyard, but it doesn't seem logical.' A heavy sigh escaped her, accompanied by a warm swell of tears that she hastily mopped with the towel, pretending to rub the front of her hair.

'I think you've been listening too much to Berd Langren,' her grandfather said as his hand rested comfortingly on her shoulder. 'I don't believe the baron is interested in the Maierstufe, not in that way. He's not so devious. You misjudge him, *Liebchen*. Hasn't it occurred to you that perhaps he's lonely? His father was a hard man, not the sort a boy could turn to. Perhaps Baron Hugo finds a substitute in me. If so, I'm glad.'

In her heart she had to agree that he was probably right. It was Berd's paranoia that made him accuse Hugo of predatory intentions toward the Maierstufe. She had never believed it. But the other things Berd had said were a different matter. She couldn't possibly confide in her grandfather about them.

'Dry your hair,' he said, dropping a kiss

on top of her head. 'And get to bed. I'll bring you some hot chocolate to help you sleep. And, *Liebchen*, I'm glad you're not a boy. I love you just as you are.'

As he left the room, another sigh heaved out of her.

With one swipe of her hand she gathered up the heather he had given her and in a surging motion carried it to the window, where she threw open the door and stepped onto the balcony with every intention of throwing the heather away. But she stopped, disconcerted by the sight of Hugo himself standing in the courtyard, with a casual jacket slung over shirt and slacks. A half moon sent silver light slanting across his upturned face. He had obviously been making for the house when he heard her window open.

'Are you all right?' he asked softly. 'I was worried. I heard what Berd Langren said, Katti, but he's wrong. I don't want the Maierstufe.'

'Oh . . . Go away, Hugo! How many times do I have to tell you? Go away and leave me alone!'

She swung back into her room, closed the window and drew the curtains across, but she couldn't shut out her memories.

In her hand she still held the crushed heather. Its branches sprang back into shape as she unclenched her fingers and stared at the plant lying in her palm. That day on the mountain he had seemed to share her sorrow. If he had been acting, he was brilliant at it. And yet today he had been devil-may-care. 'I may decide to throw discretion to the winds,' he had said, and though she had been horrified, she had loved him for it. But that, of course, was before she understood why he was being so reckless. It certainly wasn't *her* he had been thinking about.

★ ★ ★

On Sunday morning, dressed in her gray suit with a wide-brimmed hat matching her green blouse, Katarin accompanied her grandfather to church for the harvest festival service. She had attained a mood of apparent calmness, but as they approached the church gate the baronial limousine slid to a stop not far away, causing her breath to quicken. The chauffeured limousine must mean that the baroness had come to attend the service. Was Franziska with her?

Hugo climbed from the car, tall and elegant in a dark suit, and bent to help his mother alight, but they were the only passengers. Hugo's gaze met Katarin's, searching her face as the four of them exchanged polite

189

greetings and Katarin received a sharp look from the baroness.

She was relieved that, since they were not in costume, she had no need to sit by Hugo at the service, though she must be with him later for more *Weinfest* ceremonials. But as luck would have it, she found herself seated across the aisle from him, uncomfortably aware of his presence as he joined his melodious baritone in the hymns.

At the end of the service the congregation emerged into bright sunlight and stood about in animated groups. Katarin tried to hurry her grandfather away, since she had to make a quick change into her Wine Queen outfit, but before they had gone many steps Hugo said from behind them, 'May I ride up to the vineyards with you, Herr Maier? My mother will go straight back to the castle. If you would wait until I collect my costume from the car . . .'

'Of course. Of course. You're welcome, you know that.' Herr Maier glanced from one to the other of them, frowning, but decided to make no comment apart from chucking Katarin under the chin as if she were a child. 'Cheer up, *Liebchen*.'

She put on a bright smile. 'I'm perfectly cheerful *Opa*.'

Sighing, he stroked his moustache, glanced

at Hugo and moved away. 'We'd better go.'

'You're about as cheerful as a block of ice,' Hugo muttered under his breath.

'That's the way I am,' she returned in a furious undertone. 'Cold and unfeeling. Ask Berd.'

'I'm not interested in what Berd Langren thinks,' he said through his teeth, catching her arm as she tried to walk away. 'Katarin, we've got to talk!'

She shook free, glancing at the milling people around them to see if anyone had noticed — and met the unflickering gaze of the baroness, who had undoubtedly witnessed the exchange. As she caught Katarin's eye the baroness inclined her head, her expression frozen into a mask through which her eyes glinted sternly, reminding Katarin of their conversation in the Eimsee Valley. Obviously the baroness retained her suspicions and was displeased that her son should show such an interest in a little English nobody.

Stricken, Katarin started down the path in pursuit of her grandfather, with Hugo at her heels striding rapidly to catch up as she threaded her way among people sauntering to the gate.

'I wish you'd be a bit more circumspect,' she hissed at Hugo, and stretched a smile for a familiar face as she passed. 'Your mother was watching us.'

'And so?' he demanded.

She flashed him an angry look but forbore to reply. If he didn't know why he should be discreet, then now was not the time to tell him, not with so many people around. She felt in the mood for a fight.

With a little strategic timing she managed to avoid being alone with Hugo as they hurried to change into costume before driving up to the hills with Herr Maier.

In the center of the vineyards a shrine stood at the crossing of two lanes on the brow of a hill from where great stretches of vines spread, rolling down slopes and up hillsides. Parked cars lined the lanes, their occupants all heading on foot for the central spot where the priest waited.

Her red cloak fluttered as Katarin stood beside Hugo while the vineyards were solemnly blessed. The Knight of the Vine stood in position nearby and the white-clad girls were in a semicircle behind the Wine King and Queen. To one side a uniformed band stood ready to play when the brief ceremony ended; they would entertain the audience while the King and Queen made their traditional tour of the vines.

With the sound of the band blaring from

the hilltop behind them, Katarin and Hugo swept through the gateway, their cloaks billowing red and blue in the sunlight. At first Katarin's hand lay formally on Hugo's as he led her down the slope, but suddenly she felt his fingers gripping hers as if he feared she might try to escape him.

Once out of earshot of the spectators he said tautly, 'We're supposed to be encouraging the vines, not blighting them. I wish I knew what I'd done.'

'It shouldn't need explaining,' she snapped.

He lengthened his stride, practically dragging her along with him. 'You surely can't believe that I want your vineyard. That's not why — '

'I know it's not,' she gasped. 'And will you please not walk so fast? I can't keep up.'

For another few strides he kept up the pace, until they reached a connecting lane where they turned down, out of sight of the watchers on the road. With the vines almost at head height and the hump of the hill above them, they were virtually alone. A hundred yards away the band still played as it began to march down the hill to the next gate, where the Wine King and Queen would emerge.

Hugo let his supporting arm drop, his hand still fastened round hers as he turned to face her. 'Then if you didn't believe what Berd said, why did you run away? What's happened? Yesterday evening, when I came to your room — '

'Don't remind me!' she cried, looking fully at him for the first time that day. 'I'll never forgive myself for that. I almost let you make love to me. I actually thought you were sincere.'

'I was!' he said roughly, pulling her closer.

She pushed against him with all her strength as bitter suspicion broke the dam of her self-control. 'Oh, yes! You were sincerely trying to repay Franziska for flirting with Berd!'

'I was what?!' He let her go, stepped back, stared at her as though he didn't understand.

'You heard me!' Katarin raged. 'I thought it was peculiar how you were suddenly prepared to take chances, but when Berd told me what happened at the castle last Thursday — '

'Berd!' he spat the name.

'Don't deny it! He had no reason to invent such a story. You thought you'd repay her, didn't you? It didn't bother you if my reputation ended up in tatters — not to mention my feelings. You can escape. You can go back to your castle, or back to

America, and people will say what a real man Baron Hugo is. What they'll say about me doesn't bear thinking about. But you don't give a damn about that. So long as you get your own way, you don't care what it does to me. You've even used my grandfather as a means of staying around. You can't stand knowing there's one woman who would dare say no to the almighty *Herr Baron!*'

'Is that what you really believe?' he asked in a voice edged with disgust. 'That's your honest opinion of me?'

'Yes!'

A bitter laugh jerked out of him. 'Then there's nothing more to say. Obviously I've been deluding myself. I actually thought you cared about me, Katarin.'

Fancying she heard a note of pain in his voice, she searched his face, but found only chilling disdain. 'I did, for a while,' she admitted. 'And you knew it. That's why you kept pursuing me, because you thought I'd give in eventually. You might as well be honest with me now. It's all been a game, hasn't it? I've always known I could never mean anything to you.'

For a moment he was silent, a cynical light in his eyes, then he swung away and began to walk along the linkway between the vines. 'If we don't soon appear, they'll wonder what we're doing. We must think of your reputation, Fräulein Jameson.'

'It's a bit late for that,' she muttered, trudging after him.

'Oh, I think not. I'm sure no one would believe there could be anything between us. After all, I'm the Baron von Drachensberg. My family owns much land, many factories. We're aristocrats. And you . . . what are you, Fräulein Jameson, but an insignificant girl with pretensions to run one of the major vineyards in the valley? A foreigner. An upstart.'

Hating him, she cast a bleak glance at the arrogant way he held himself as he strode just ahead of her, the cloak flowing from broad shoulders, the crown set squarely on unruly dark hair. He stopped so suddenly that she almost bumped into him, drawing back a little as he whirled on her, his face dark with rage.

'Is that what you think? Answer me, Katarin! You think I calmly set out to seduce you, just for the hell of it?'

She had seen him angry before, but never quite that angry, his eyes wintry as blizzards in a face gone craggy. It gave her pause, made her wonder if she had been wrong.

'Not . . . not intentionally, perhaps,' she muttered.

'Oh, yes. Yes! You're accusing me of cold-bloodedly plotting seduction. Did that idea come from Berd Langren, too? Why do you always listen to him? Why won't you believe *me*?'

'I don't know what to believe!' she yelled at him, and turned away as tears burst from her eyes. 'Oh, damn!' she muttered, flinging an arm across her face.

After a moment's silence Hugo said quietly from behind her, 'You'll spoil your makeup. Here, use my handkerchief.'

Soft linen came against her fingers and she used it to dry her tears carefully, ashamed of the stupid scene she was making and horribly aware that, up on the hill, everyone would be waiting for them to appear.

'Perhaps it's time I did speak up,' he said softly. 'I've been keeping quiet because I didn't want to put pressure on you. I've already been unfair, I know that. But all's fair in love and war. Isn't that what they say?'

'And which is this?' she croaked.

'A little of both, maybe. Look at me, Katarin.'

Unwillingly she lifted her head and found him regarding her with his head on one side and a rueful light in his eyes. 'You look as though you're willing me to drop dead,' he said. 'You've blotched your makeup. I told

197

you that you would. May I?' He took the handkerchief from her and gently wiped a smear of mascara from near her eye. 'There, that's better. By the time we reach the gate you'll be recovered.' Hoisting his robe, he put the handkerchief back in his trouser pocket and took her hand. 'We'll walk steadily. I'll talk and you listen for once. Is that agreed?'

'I'll listen,' she said dully, 'but I can't guarantee it will make any difference.'

They began to walk fairly slowly, ranks of vines passing on either side like lines of soldiers on parade weighed down by golden fruit. She felt exhausted, as though the whole thing was a nightmare. The only reality was a strong hand clasped warmly round hers by a man she detested — a man on whom she wanted to lean for comfort. Madness!

'It's true I discovered Franziska with Berd at the castle,' he informed her levelly.

'And that you were furious,' she added.

'Yes, I was. But to understand why, you have to understand how things have been between Franziska and me.'

'I know how they've been,' she said dully.

His hand tightened, making her wince. 'I asked you to listen. Have the courtesy not to keep interrupting, please . . . I've known Franziska for most of her life. She's

198

fourteen years younger than I am, so I've always thought of her as a child. It's what she still is — a little spoiled brat. But . . . well, our families have been very close friends. A joining by marriage seemed a pleasant idea.'

'In this day and age?' she asked in disbelief. 'An arrangement?'

He gave her a reproving look. 'Not quite as definite as that. Just a pleasant idea that our parents thought of many years ago. And it might have worked, if Franziska and I had had anything in common. Until I came home for my father's funeral, I hadn't seen her for some time. Suddenly she was grown up. I believe, for a while, I did entertain vague intentions toward her. That was before I knew her. She's a tiresome little beast. You must have seen that yourself. And she doesn't like *me* much, either.'

'Then why — ' she began hotly, and stopped as he gave her a quelling look.

'Why were we engaged?' he finished for her. 'We never were, not officially.'

He paused a moment to let that fact percolate her stunned brain, then threw out a hand in a gesture of futility. 'Did you ever ask me about her? No, you listened to gossip. Oh, I know my mother took things for granted. Even Franziska seemed ready to go along with it, for the sake of my name and my title. I suspect her father's influence in that. Having a daughter married to one of the big industrial names might help his political career, but for Franziska and myself, personally, it would have been a farce. There was no way I could have been persuaded. Twice now my mother has invited Franziska to stay, probably hoping she could make me change my mind. The first time she came was that weekend when you arrived to invite me to be Wine King. The second time was for the hunt. That's all. I've seen more of *you* than I've seen of her lately.'

'She stuck to you pretty closely,' Katarin observed, not entirely convinced.

'In public, yes. But it was only for show. In private she's hardly civil to me. She's always bored and restless. Which is why she encouraged Berd, I suppose. If I was angry when I found them it was partly on his account. I know very well how tempting Franziska can be when she tries. But she was also under my protection. What she does in her father's house I'm not sure, but I wasn't going to have her seduced in *my* house, by Berd or by anyone else.'

'I see,' she said faintly, hardly knowing how to take this news. She would need a chance to think back and decide just what it meant, since in believing him to be engaged to Franziska she had misinterpreted all his actions.

They were approaching the junction of lanes that would bring them within sight of the road, from where the band could still be heard playing. Hugo drew Katarin to a standstill, looking down at her with a little frown.

'Franziska and I had a long talk and agreed there was no point in keeping our families in suspense any longer. We're not suited to each other in any way, and if we had had any sense, we would have seen that long ago. So, now you know. Should I have told you before?'

'I'm not sure. Perhaps you should. I've thought some terrible things about you.'

'You've said them, too,' he reminded her, a smile tugging at a corner of his mouth as he laid his hands on either side of her face. 'There's one thing more I want to tell you. Maybe I shouldn't, but I'm tired of trying to be fair and honorable. Katarin . . . I love you.'

She felt as though she had been struck by lightning, delight and dismay shivering through her in equal amounts. 'Don't say that!'

'I shan't repeat it,' he assured her, the

smile dying, leaving his face strained and somber. 'I just wanted you to know, because I believe you feel something for me, too, and I can't just let it go, however much you beg me to leave you alone. Whatever promises you've made to your Englishman, surely you'll give yourself time to find out how you really feel?'

Her mouth trembled, but no words would come. She had forgotten telling him about the 'man in her life.' Was that why he had held back — because he believed *she* was not free? Was that what he meant about being fair?

She managed to say, 'Hugo . . . ' and then he was kissing her tenderly, holding her face as if it were a delicate flower while his lips moved softly on hers, calling a response from depths that had never been tapped before. So intense was the feeling that it frightened her, bringing thoughts of all the complications that loving him must bring — David, *Opa*, the baroness, Berd, the people of Gundelheim . . . Everyone would be against them.

She drew away from him, finding that she was weeping again. 'We mustn't, Hugo. We really mustn't. It's no good.'

'Very well,' he said gravely, fishing for his handkerchief. 'If that's how you feel, I won't kiss you again. It only makes you cry. Here, use this, *Liebling*. And forgive me.'

'It's not your fault,' she sobbed. 'Really it's not. It's me. I'm such a fool.'

'No, *Liebling*.'

'Yes!' She lifted a distraught face. 'And please don't call me *Liebling*.'

'But it's what you are — my darling, my love. Since we first met on the mountain — '

'*Herr Baron?*' a voice called, alarmingly close at hand.

She exchanged a horrified glance with Hugo in the second before Herr Brach's ample figure appeared, coming to find them. He owned the vineyard they were in. Presumably he had been sent to see what had happened.

He took one look at Katarin's tear-stained face and leaped to conclusions, turning a dull beet red as he cleared his throat. 'Ahem . . . excuse me. We, er . . . we were anxious in case something might have gone wrong.'

'That's very kind of you,' Hugo said smoothly. 'Yes, we have had a mishap. Fräulein Jameson stumbled and twisted her ankle. I've been carrying her and we stopped so that I could take a breather. I believe it's only a sprain, but it's very painful, isn't it, Katarin?'

'Oh — oh, yes.' Gathering her scrambled

wits, she effected a painful limp and an overbalance, grasping Hugo's arm for support. Without hesitation he bent and swept her up into his arms, looking concerned.

'I told you not to put your weight on it. Hold on. We'll soon get you to the car.'

Katarin was never sure whether the pantomime convinced Herr Brach, but he seemed ready enough to go along with it. He walked alongside, murmuring appropriately sympathetic words, as she folded her arms round Hugo's neck and rested on his broad shoulder, looking through tear-wet lashes at his tanned profile while her apricot hair fanned across his cloak. Her imagination took flight and she restrained it with an audible gasp that made him look into her face, his expression at once fierce and tender.

'Is it hurting?' he asked solicitously.

'It's agony,' she replied in English, and knew that he understood she was not referring to her perfectly undamaged ankle.

9

Bad as she felt about it, the deception had to continue as, to the concern of everyone present, Hugo tenderly set her in the back of her grandfather's car and sat beside her for the drive to their house, all the time assuring her grandfather that the damage was minimal. He then conveyed her from the car to the sitting room, where he took charge of the situation by suggesting that Herr Maier might make them all some coffee while he, Hugo, applied a bandage to Katarin's ankle with as much care as if she had really been hurt. But at least it prevented her grandfather from seeing that she was unbruised and not even slightly swollen.

'You're a terrible liar,' she breathed when her grandfather left the room.

'I thought I was rather good at it,' Hugo replied with a crooked smile. 'Anyway, you can't accuse me of not caring about your reputation in this instance. I trust we've allayed any suspicions.'

'Unless Herr Brach talks. He wasn't entirely convinced. You don't suppose he heard what we were saying, do you?'

He sat back on his heels, frowning at her. 'I'm not sure. But in any case it can't be helped. We'll just have to take care not to give them cause for any further gossip. The bandage isn't too tight, is it?'

'No, it's fine, thank you.'

He stretched to his full height as Herr Maier returned to ask if he would stay for lunch.

'I won't, thank you,' Hugo replied. 'Do you mind if I leave my costume here until tomorrow evening?'

'Not at all. But how will you get back to the castle? Your mother took the limousine. If I can give you a lift — '

'That's very kind of you, but I'll go up by the railway and through the woods. There's a place there, not far below the castle. A waterfall, not easy to find. Do you know it?'

Herr Maier shook his head. 'No, I don't think so. I've only been up in those woods a few times, though Katarin likes to go there. But you were saying . . . this waterfall?'

'Oh . . . nothing, really, I think it must have been a shrine, maybe to a pagan god. It's very old. So' — a small gesture, a deprecatory smile — 'you'll think me superstitious, but I go there when I need to feel at peace, or if I've something special to wish for. I can't think why I mentioned it. Good-bye for now, Herr Maier. Take care of that ankle, Katarin.'

And he was gone.

Lying on the settee, Katarin thought about the grotto. It was odd that Hugo should think of it as a special place, too. She knew very well why he had mentioned it — as a message for her. Little imagination was needed to guess what he might be wishing for.

But the granting of that wish was as impossible now as it had been before. To begin with, she was still tied to David, if only tenuously. And even when that problem had been dealt with there remained everything else, barrier after barrier.

Despite the heart-searching, she knew that if Hugo came that night to carry her off to an elopement, she would go with him gladly. She only feared that she didn't have the courage to take the final step for herself.

★ ★ ★

Round and round the thoughts went for the rest of that day and half into the night, so that when eventually she did fall asleep she slept dreamlessly, deeply, until she was shocked awake by the tolling of all the church bells in the town.

Lord! The harvest!

As she jumped out of bed a tractor revved up in the yard and she was in time to see her grandfather drive out, with Ernst and Gody and several other people perched precariously on the edges of the trailer, which bore a selection of old barrels for the grapes to be collected in. In the road half the town was on the move, men, women, and children, all equipped with vine-cutters, streaming out in clear morning sunlight.

Hastily Katarin scrambled into some clothes and ran down the stairs to the kitchen, where Frau Grainau was preparing a breakfast tray.

'Why on earth didn't someone wake me?' Katarin demanded as the housekeeper looked up in astonishment.

'But your ankle!'

'My . . . oh . . . yes. But it's much better. Much better, really. I can't miss the harvest. Stick a couple of rolls in a lunch box, would you, please? I'll just have a quick coffee and then I'll be off.'

Katarin soon found her grandfather giving instructions to a group of students who had come to help. He expressed surprise at seeing her and she was obliged to repeat that her ankle was better. She was assigned a row to pick, given a basket to strap round her shoulders, and with eager hands she began the task of removing bunches of grapes cleanly with sharp scissors, dropping them over her shoulder into the basket until it became too heavy to carry.

Shoulders aching under the weight of her basket, she made her way to the nearest grassed lane and deposited her load in a half-full cask, where it was swiftly inspected by the checker. When the cask overflowed with fruit it would be heaved up onto a trailer. Soon tractors were buzzing to and fro, taking grapes back to the pressing rooms and returning with empty casks to be refilled.

By lunchtime, which was announced by a sharp whistle that screamed all over the vineyard, Katarin's back was stiff and her hands sore, but she felt a wonderful sense of achievement. Judging by the look on his face as he joined her for a picnic lunch on the grass, her grandfather felt the same.

'We've done it, *Liebchen*.' He grinned beneath his moustache. 'It's wonderful having you to share it with me. At last I've got someone who cares about the Maierstufe as much as I do.'

But for Katarin a small cloud sullied the day. The Maierstufe, much as she loved it, would deny her her dearest dream. How could she betray her grandfather by marrying

Hugo? Wondering where Hugo was, she glanced up at the castle on its crag above the valley. Was he in his own vineyard, sharing a picnic lunch with his own pickers? Or was he away in Stuttgart on business connected with his factories? Was he thinking about her, too?

'You'll see him tonight,' her grandfather's soft voice broke across her thoughts, making her flush.

'See whom?'

'Berd Langren, of course,' he said dryly. 'Whom did you think I meant — St. Nicholas? 'See whom,' indeed.'

So he knew; he knew something. 'Has he . . . said anything to you?'

'Who, Berd? Or St. Nicholas?'

Flustered by his teasing, she glanced at the people nearby, lowering her voice. 'You know whom I mean!'

'Do I?'

'*Opa*!'

Chuckling, he heaved himself to his knees and then to his feet, lifting the whistle that hung round his neck. 'We'll have to talk about it later, *Liebchen*. It's time to get back to work.'

★ ★ ★

By the time the church bells rang out their message that a mist was rising to dew the grapes and everyone must stop picking, Katarin's body was one massive ache. She wondered how she would ever cope with the dance that, as Wine Queen, she had to attend that night. She and most of the other pickers hitched a lift on half empty trailers as the last few loads of grapes trundled home to be pressed.

Having eaten a meal and rested for a while, she took a soothing hot bath that helped to loosen her muscles before she donned the paneled gown and the velvet cloak.

'Are you ready, Katti?' her grandfather called, tapping on her door. When she looked out to show him she was dressed, he grinned approval and said in a confidential tone, 'He's here. St. Nicholas.'

Though her heart jumped and began to beat at twice its normal speed, she managed to give him a look that reproved his teasing. 'I'll be right down.'

Carrying her crown in one hand, she followed her grandfather down the stairs and into the sitting room, where Hugo was fastening the blue cloak over his red robe. His discarded jacket lay across the back of a chair and his hair looked disheveled.

A speaking glance flashed between them

211

in the instant before he said pleasantly, 'Good evening, Katarin. I hope your ankle's better.'

'Much better,' she said.

Beside her, her grandfather smoothed his moustache with a gnarled forefinger, murmuring, 'She made a miraculous recovery. Well, if you'll excuse me, I have work in the cellars. Enjoy yourselves.'

When he had gone Hugo came to take the gilded crown from her hand and set it on her head, then caught her hands in his as he looked down at her seriously. 'You look tired. Your grandfather said you'd been picking grapes all day.'

'We need every pair of hands we can get,' she replied.

He glanced down at the hands he held, turning them over to study her roughened skin, the blisters, and the cut on one finger. Despite a soaking in lotion her hands looked a mess and she was ashamed of them, but when she tried to pull away he only held her tighter.

'You should wear gloves,' he said. 'You've cut yourself.' And he lifted her hand to press his lips to the small injury, watching her face. 'The vineyard's very important to you, isn't it?'

'Yes, it is.'

'I knew that on the day of the storm,' he told her. 'But a vineyard is only a vineyard, Katti. To give your life to it would be a waste.'

'I don't think so,' she said, and twisted free of his grasp. 'We ought to go. Where's your crown?'

'Here, somewhere.' He found it half under one of the cushions on the settee and stood before a mirror on the wall, straightening his hair with his fingers before fitting the crown on his head, frowning at his reflection.

'It's not just a vineyard, anyway,' Katarin said. 'It's the Maierstufe. I don't expect you to understand, but that piece of land, and the vines on it, have been cultivated by Maiers for nearly two centuries. To me, it's . . . it's something I was born to, the way you were born to your castle. It's part of me.'

Turning his head, he gave her a long, speculative look and said simply, 'Yes, I know. Shall we go?'

The dance was being held in a beer cellar beneath one of the inns, a cavelike place full of noise and whirling lights. A group of masked young people met the Wine King and Queen and led them to their table above the dance floor, where couples gyrated to the rhythm of music played by an energetic group on the dais.

For a while they tried to hold a shouted conversation with their hosts, but the noise made it such an effort that, eventually, they gave up, laughing, and one of the girls unceremoniously dragged Hugo onto the floor to dance.

'You, too, Your Majesty,' a young man yelled in Katarin's ear, taking her hand.

Her protesting muscles soon loosened up as she twisted and swayed in the middle of the crowd, colored light shifting over masks and sweating faces, some of them laughing, some intensely serious. From across the floor she caught Hugo's eye, seeing him lift a humorous eyebrow, and even at that distance her stomach knotted in response to him. She wondered what his mother would have thought to see her aristocratic son dancing energetically with the best of them.

Perhaps two hours later, when the heat and the noise were becoming almost too much to stand, Hugo managed to convey to her that they had done their duty and might leave without causing offense. They escaped eventually, amid much laughter and cheerful leg-pulling, reaching the night air with relief only to be swept up by a group of revelers on their way to the square and carried along with them.

'At this rate we'll be on our knees by

the end of the week,' Hugo said as they stood refreshing themselves with wine from one of the booths, with music jangling from a nearby merry-go-round and the scent of cooking sausages filling the air. 'You're not cold, are you?'

She shook her head. 'No, this cloak's lovely and warm.'

'Too warm,' he said wryly. 'It's all right for you, but I'm fully dressed under this damn robe. I was beginning to think I was melting in the *Bierkeller*. And I'll never understand how you women manage in skirts. This thing keeps getting in my way.'

'You shouldn't stride out so much.'

'You want me to mince about?' he demanded.

Laughing, Katarin said, 'You look wonderful just as you are. Very imposing. Very regal.'

'Thank you.' All at once he was serious, looking at her with such longing that her heart turned over. 'And you . . . are beautiful.'

Her head swam, from wine and from conflicting emotions, but before she could reply they were accosted by some visitors wanting to know all about the *Weinfest* traditions. Katarin's exertions began to make themselves felt. Her legs ached and her head throbbed.

'Do you think we could go home?' she

asked of Hugo as the tourists moved away. 'We aren't expected to stay all night, are we?'

'I think it's enough that we put in an appearance,' he replied, taking her arm to lead her to where he had left his car.

She sank gratefully into the soft suede seat, closing her eyes and letting her head loll.

'You're tired out,' Hugo said softly. 'You must take things more easily tomorrow. The harvest will come in without you exerting yourself too much. What is it tomorrow evening — a concert?'

'At the school. That should be less energetic, thank heaven.'

'And on Wednesday?'

'No official engagements on Wednesday. You can take a day off from your skirts.'

In the dimness of the car she saw him smile as he lifted a hand to brush her cheek very lightly.

'Hugo . . . ' There was something she had to know. 'Are you planning to go back to America?'

'Not permanently. I've appointed another manager for our factory there. Now that my father's gone, I've taken his place as head of all the Drachensberg concerns. Most of my work can be done from home, with occasional visits to Stuttgart, or Bonn — or to America. Why do you ask?'

'I just wondered.'

'Are you interested in my future?' he asked in a low voice. 'I shall be around, don't worry. If you need me, you'll only have to call.'

Feeling the sting of tears, Katarin turned her head away, and after a moment's silence he started the car and drove her home.

Lights still blazing from the pressing rooms told of continued activity there as grapes from the day's harvest were stripped and crushed before going into the great hydraulic presses, from where their juice went down into huge vats in the cellars to be treated and left to ferment.

'I'll just come in and get changed,' Hugo said as they left the car in the courtyard. 'This robe could do with a wash.'

'Mine, too,' she agreed. 'I'll ask Frau Grainau to do them tomorrow, or I'll do them myself.'

In the sitting room she watched as he unfastened his heavy cloak and laid it across a chair before stripping off the robe, beneath which he wore a T-shirt and slacks. There was something curiously intimate about the process, about seeing the way his hair tousled as he emerged from the robe, shook it out and laid it aside before picking up his jacket, shrugging into it. Then he went to the mirror and combed his hair, turning to give her a smile that was both rueful and regretful.

'Until tomorrow evening, then.'

Unable to speak for the surge of tears in her throat, she nodded, and didn't attempt to avoid him as he came and took her face between his hands, bending to kiss her firmly but briefly.

'You said you wouldn't do that,' she reminded him hoarsely.

'I know,' he replied in a tense undertone. 'And once I said I'd never touch you again unless you begged me, and I also said I wouldn't keep telling you that I love you. But I can't help myself, Katarin. I'm here and your Englishman is far away. If I take unfair advantage of his absence, then believe it's because I want you very much. He should come here. He shouldn't leave you alone. If you were mine, I'd never let you out of my sight, no, not for a moment. I'd be too afraid that someone else might look at you and love you. Either he trusts you too much, or he doesn't care what you do. Which is it?'

'It's not as simple as that,' she croaked, blinking at a veil of tears. 'It's not just David. It's everything else. Your mother . . . '

'What about my mother?'

'Nothing.' Gently she took hold of his

wrists and eased his hands away from her before turning away. 'I don't know. I can't seem to think straight. When you're here — ' She bit the words off, afraid of committing herself too deeply at a moment when she was vulnerable, when the wine had given her false courage.

'Am I making things difficult for you?' he asked.

'Yes,' she sighed. 'Yes, you are.'

'Good.'

Wondering if she had heard right, she glanced round at him. 'What?'

'I said, 'Good,' ' he informed her.

'You mean you're glad you're making things difficult?' she asked in disbelief.

'Oh, yes. Oh, yes, *Liebling*.' Softly coming very close to her, he drew her into his arms, smiling down at her bewilderment. 'Because it means you aren't indifferent to me, you see? And perhaps if I make things very, very difficult, you might stop fighting it.'

The way he kissed her then made things even more difficult, for though her head had reservations, her heart, her body, and her senses were all on his side. Breathless, she leaned against him, her arms twined round his neck, her face against the warm brown curve of his throat.

'*Liebling*,' he said softly. 'Now you are

making difficulties for me. I'm not made of stone.'

'Neither am I,' she breathed.

Hard hands suddenly fierce on her waist forced her away from him and she looked up, startled, to see his face grim with anger. 'If you think I'd be satisfied just having you as my mistress you're wrong, Katarin! I want more. Much more.'

'I didn't mean . . .' Her voice trailed off because she wasn't sure exactly what she had meant, except that she loved being close to him, warm in his arms.

'No, perhaps not,' he conceded, though his frown remained. 'Not here in your grandfather's house when he may come in at any moment. But in case any doubts remain we may as well have it clear. I don't want a few minutes of stolen pleasure. Not from you. I want everything. I want the rest of your life. Unless you can offer me that, I'll take nothing of you. You understand?'

Shaken by the intensity in him, she swallowed hard and said, 'Yes, I understand. But you must know that we can't, Hugo. We can't!'

'Stop being so negative,' he chided. 'We can, if it's what we both want. It's what *I* want, Katarin. I'm only waiting for you to make up your mind.'

220

He kissed her again, slowly, tenderly, and left before she had recovered enough breath to speak. She found herself trembling, a hand exploring the soft swell of her lips. Feeling the roughness of her work-worn fingers, she stared at her hands, seeing them blistered and cut — hardly the hands of a woman fit to marry a baron. But that was what he had been suggesting. 'The rest of your life,' he had said. And he was right. An affair wouldn't be enough. Not for them. It had to be everything.

★ ★ ★

The next day, at her grandfather's insistence, she stayed away from the Maierstufe and spent her time in the pressing rooms and cellars, helping Fritz keep an eye on the mashing and pressing processes and watching the grape juice, or 'must,' as it was treated with necessary chemicals and left to stand and ferment. And she had the pleasure of tasting some of the new young wine as it emerged still fizzy, white with sediment from grape flesh and skins.

In the courtyard tractors droned to and fro, bringing loads of fresh grapes and departing with empty casks, and occasionally a wine tanker nosed through the gates to collect the must, which would be treated in the vast cellars of the cooperative, where wines from the whole valley were blended. Only the very best of the Maierstufe produce, carefully selected by Herr Maier, his granddaughter, and their cellar master, was kept to be processed on the home premises.

The evening concert proved to be an entertaining affair, a blend of music and amateur dramatics. Although Katarin had little private conversation with Hugo, she was left in no doubt that he was still waiting, with growing impatience, for her to decide what she wished to do. Since she remained confused she was grateful for her grandfather's presence on the drive back to the house. Hugo had coffee with them, but returned to the castle immediately afterwards, contenting himself with snatching a kiss from her in the darkened courtyard.

She had begun to feel that he was pressuring her a little too strongly and she was not sorry that Wednesday would give her a break from his disturbing presence.

She spent that midweek day taking a turn at driving the tractor to and from the Maierstufe, and she would have spent the evening working in the cellars if her grandfather hadn't shooed her out to rest. Putting her feet up on the settee, she tried to relax and watch television, but though she was physically tired, her mind went round in circles, all centered on Hugo.

She had thought she needed a break, but she missed him with a sick yearning that was new to her. The twenty-four hours that must pass before she saw him again stretched in front of her like a yawning chasm. But she also realized there was one step she could take.

She went up to her room and wrote to David, telling him as gently as she could that she loved someone else. She apologized for having kept him in suspense for so long, but now it was very clear to her that she had to be honest and release him from their understanding.

She experienced a surprising sense of relief when the letter was finished, sealed and stamped, propped on the side of her dressing table opposite to where Hugo's heather stood in its vase. At least she had resolved one of her problems; she had been honest with David.

★ ★ ★

Hugo arrived the following evening as darkness was falling and together they went down to the mill, where the riverside was

223

strung with lights and tables and chairs were set beneath the trees. Canoe races took place on the river, and a barge decorated like a swan gave rides around a nearby island in honor of the fabled Lohengrin. After awhile Gundelheim's Knight of the Vine was said to have been based on one of Lohengrin's companions.

Beneath the trees people ate and drank, or wandered from group to group chatting and laughing, while the Wine King and his Queen were required to circulate, as usual, dispensing wine and jollity as they went. Katarin wondered if she should say that she had written to David, but decided that the news could wait until later. Too many people surrounded them, seeming determined to keep her and Hugo apart for once.

'I'll have some of that,' a familiar voice said and Katarin turned to find Berd holding up a glass that she filled from the bottle she was holding.

'Where have you been all week?' she asked.

'I've been around. I've seen you if you haven't seen me. I've been watching you — you and him. Pretty cozy, aren't you?'

She glanced at the people around her, but none of them seemed to be taking any notice of Berd, for which she was thankful. 'Look, Berd — '

'No, *you* look,' he interrupted fiercely. 'Look at yourself. You're letting him make a complete fool of you. He's got the whole town round his little finger now, but it's you and your grandfather who are most tightly entwined in his coils.'

'Oh, not again!' She sighed. 'I'm sick of listening to this. You're like a record with a stuck needle. Let's get to the root of this, shall we? What did he ever do to you?'

For a moment he regarded her with dull fury, his mouth bunched in stubborn lines, then he turned on his heel and marched away, throwing his wineglass down with such force that it smashed against a tree. Katarin watched him, worried by his continued animosity, until he disappeared among the trees.

'What did he say?' Hugo asked, materializing beside her.

'Oh, much the same as always. I wish he'd grow up. He worries me.'

'Why?'

'Why?' she echoed, turning to him. 'Because I'm afraid he might do something . . . I don't know what. But something to hurt you.'

'Words can't hurt me,' he said, taking her hand firmly in his own. 'Put down that bottle and let's take a walk. I need a few minutes' respite.'

She set the bottle on the nearest table, laughing and telling the people who sat there that it was a gift from the Wine Queen; then she allowed Hugo to lead her to where lights faded into shadows among the trees and there was space to breathe and talk privately, with the river flowing by.

'I don't think you need trouble yourself about Berd,' Hugo said quietly. 'I don't expect to be liked by everyone. But it's nice to know you worry about me.'

'Of course I worry about you!' she said sharply. 'You're . . . you're important to me.'

Smiling to himself, he looked down at their joined hands, a thumb stroking her knuckles. 'On the morning of the hunt,' he told her, 'Berd said . . . He was telling your grandfather, but everyone heard and I'm sure it was meant for me. He said that you had told him you were going to marry your Englishman.'

'Yes, that's true,' she replied and, when his head came up sharply, 'I mean it's true that I said it, not that I meant it.'

'I know. I met your grandfather the next day and he informed me what you'd said. You lied, to discourage Berd.'

Peering at him in the indistinct light, she said slowly, '*Opa* told you?'

'He did. Why do you think I was so happy on Saturday, when we met to start the *Fest*? I knew you were unsure of your Englishman and I thought perhaps if I made a determined assault on your heart I might have a chance. You thought I was being reckless, but it wasn't that. And it had nothing to do with Franziska flirting with Berd. I was simply trying to get through those stout defenses. How am I succeeding?'

'Too well, if you want the truth.'

'Then what's the problem? If it's what I said in the wine museum that day, about wine-making being a man's job . . . I didn't really mean that. I didn't know how much it meant to you then.'

'Maybe not, but . . . ' Over his shoulder she saw two figures approaching, outlined against the lights that illumined the party. One of them looked like Berd. She saw him point in her direction, heard him say in English, 'There she is, see?' The other man came on, lifting a hand to brush aside a low branch.

As Hugo glanced round to see what had so captured her attention, the newcomer came close enough for her to recognize him, even in half-darkness with lights blazing behind him. She knew that slender figure, the close-cropped curling hair, even before he said, in English, with a little gesture of apology, 'Hello, Katie. You sent for me, so I've come.'

'David!' she breathed.

Beside her, Hugo made a move as if to walk away, but she clasped his hand tighter. 'No, don't . . . '

He looked down at her, his face drained and weary. 'I think I must, Katti. You're the one who must decide.' Withdrawing his hand, he walked unhurriedly away, passing David with a nod and a murmured, '*Guten Abend*,' leaving Katarin shaking and uncertain. Just when she needed him most, he had deserted her.

10

'Who's that?' David asked.

'That's . . . His name's Hugo. He's my Wine King.' Her eyes followed the tall, cloaked figure as he stepped back among the lights and was immediately surrounded by revelers.

'Even I could see that,' David said. 'I don't suppose he normally goes around robed and crowned. Impressive, isn't he? You, too. I'm sorry if I came at a bad moment, but I ran into Berd and he brought me here.'

With an effort she brought her mind back to the man beside her. 'You've . . . just arrived?'

'Half an hour ago. I hired a car at the airport. I suppose I should have written, but I wasn't sure I could get away until the last minute. You did say you wanted to talk to me. It sounded pretty important.'

Realizing that she couldn't say what she had to say there beside the river in the darkness, she asked, 'Where's your car now?'

'Up on the road. Are you allowed to leave?'

'I don't suppose it will matter. We'll go

back to *Opa*'s. You'll be staying?'

'Just overnight. That's all I can manage.'

The house was deserted, so presumably her grandfather had gone down to the cellars with Fritz. She gave David a drink, then escaped to her own room to change out of her cloak and gown into a sweater and skirt, all the time wondering what Hugo would be thinking.

David was in the sitting room, adjusting the hands of the cuckoo clock, which was a minute or two slow. On the low table his glass of wine stood untouched.

'Don't you like the wine?' she asked.

He glanced round, hands deep in the pockets of his travel-creased slacks. 'I'd prefer a beer, if you've got one. You know I'm not much of a wine-drinker.'

That was something she had forgotten, as she had forgotten the engaging way his hair crinkled, crisp and nut-brown, and the slouching way he held his tall thinness, not straight and proud like Hugo. It occurred to her that if she had met Hugo first she would not have looked twice at David, or any other man.

She poured him a beer and sipped the wine herself, sitting tensely on the edge of a chair opposite him. 'Well . . . '

'You haven't said you're pleased to see

me,' David said with a thin smile. 'No, don't bother. As a matter of fact I've been thinking for some time that I really ought to come and see you. The situation is ridiculous. I gather you're not prepared to come back to England, so — '

'You gather — from whom?'

Pursing his lips, he turned his beer mug in circles. 'Carol, actually.'

'Carol Masters? I didn't realize you knew her.'

'I didn't, but she called round at my flat because she'd lost your address and . . . ' His face twisted and he glanced across at her. 'I'm sorry to have to tell you this, Katie, but I've been seeing rather a lot of her over the past three months. When she came over for that holiday she was going to try and tell you about us, but . . . '

As he stared at her unhappily her mind jumped back six weeks, to a day in August and Carol saying, 'I've found someone rather special. Don't ask me about him.'

'You mean you're serious about each other?' she said slowly. 'She did talk about getting married.'

'That's right. Probably next Easter. Katie . . . I'm sorry.'

'Don't be,' she said with a sigh, a weight shifting from her shoulders even while she

231

struggled with a sense of betrayal. Carol had visited her, had even asked about David, without giving any clue to her own feelings for him. 'David, I'm happy for you. For both of you. I wish she'd had the guts to tell me, though. She had every opportunity.'

'She was worried about upsetting you,' he replied. 'Besides, it was really my job to break the news. Thanks for taking it like this.'

'What did you expect — hysterics? Actually, David, I . . . I wanted us to talk because . . . I've found someone else, too. It's funny, but only yesterday I wrote and told you about it. You'll probably find the letter waiting when you get home.'

After a moment he afforded her a wry smile. 'So it did happen. Carol said it might. She quite fancied him herself, you know.'

Misinterpreting the look on her face, he added swiftly, 'Oh, she's quite open about things like that. But, as she says herself, marrying me won't stop her noticing other men, it will just stop her doing anything about it. It's odd, though. He seemed quite pleased to see me. He didn't mind my talking to you.'

'Who didn't?' she said blankly.

'Berd Langren. Isn't that who it is?'

'No. No, it's not. Certainly not. Oh,

David, will you excuse me? I must go back to the river. *Opa* should be in soon, and there's plenty more beer in the fridge. And food. Help yourself, will you?'

But down by the river the party was almost over, only a few people remaining to clear up the worst of the debris. She received some odd looks when she asked for Hugo. The *Herr Baron* had gone home some time ago, she was informed. It had been assumed that she had gone with him.

Despairing, Katarin drove more slowly back through a town beginning to settle down for the night. Even the market square was almost deserted. She had not realized how late it was.

She discovered David with her grandfather, who had obviously been having celebrations of his own in the cellar with Fritz Kurtze. He was barely capable of standing upright, let alone holding a serious conversation. Scolding, she dispatched him to bed and wondered if she dared phone the castle.

'I should leave it,' David advised. 'It's past midnight, you know. He's probably gone to bed. He surely can't believe that my turning up will make any difference. If he was all that anxious, he'd have phoned you.'

Would he? Katarin wondered.

By morning, however, after a sleepless,

miserable night, she could no longer wait to talk to Hugo. After her grandfather had gone to the vineyard and while David was still sleeping, she telephoned the castle and, to her consternation, found herself talking with the baroness.

'May I speak with Hugo, please?' she asked in a small voice. 'It's Katarin Jameson.'

'Ah, Fräulein Jameson!' came the bright reply. 'How good of you to call. How are you? And your grandfather, Herr Maier? . . . Good, good. No, I'm sorry to have to tell you that my son is not here. He's on his way to Stuttgart for a business meeting. I don't expect him home before this evening, and probably quite late. May I give him a message?'

'No, thank you. Just . . . tell him I called, would you, please? Thank you.'

Gone to Stuttgart, she thought dully. And probably wouldn't be home until late. Then what about the men's night he was due to attend that evening? What about the ball tomorrow?

It was odd that the baroness had sounded so friendly. Much too friendly, actually, all sweetness and civility. In the bleak mood that depressed her that morning, Katarin fancied that civility from the baroness boded no good for her and Hugo. Suppose his mother didn't pass on the message?

'Oh, come on, now,' David said when she confided her troubles to him. 'The old girl can't be that bad.'

'You don't know her,' she said. 'I've got a feeling she'd do anything to keep us apart. Not that we're ever likely to get together, the way things are going. He's marvelous, but I can't marry him. It wouldn't be fair to *Opa*.'

'Yes, well, I'm afraid I don't really understand what your grandfather and his vineyard have got to do with it. Good grief, you've got this stinking rich bloke begging you to marry him. What on earth's stopping you?'

'Maybe the fact that he's stinking rich,' as you so elegantly put it. 'If he were ordinary, there wouldn't be any problem.'

'Well, you'll have to sort it out for yourself, love. If I don't go, I'll miss my plane.'

She saw him off, told him to give her love to Carol, and then immersed herself in the cellars among the alcoholic aromas of the fermenting must. At least the Maierstufe hadn't failed her.

★ ★ ★

The day seemed endless, the evening even longer. Her grandfather went off quite late to join the stag party in the *Bierkeller*, and Katarin, not knowing where Hugo was, in Stuttgart or in Gundelheim, took herself to bed and lay curled in a tight ball hugging her pillow. She did not expect to rest, but eventually sleep dropped over her like a black blanket and the next thing she knew it was Saturday morning, with the sun angling across her curtains.

She found her grandfather in the kitchen mixing some vile concoction in a glass while Frau Grainau looked on askance.

'Had another heavy night, did you?' Katarin asked. '*Opa*, was Hugo there?'

He glanced round, surprisingly bright-eyed and alert. 'Of course he was. One can't have a men's night without the Wine King. Here, you'd better take him this. I've got work to do.'

She stared at the glassful of whatever it was, and at him. He looked bland, but a twinkle danced in his eye.

'He's here?' she said. 'Hugo's here?'

'In the spare room. I daren't let him drive, the state he was in. He and Berd drowned a lot of sorrows last night.'

'He . . . and Berd?' She didn't believe it.

'Yes, yes. *Liebchen*, stop gaping like a stranded salmon and take him this. He'll probably need it. Frau Grainau will make him some breakfast. And see that he eats it.'

He thrust the glass into her hand and stalked out. Bewildered, Katarin exchanged a glance with the housekeeper, who shrugged and said, 'Oh, men! They're all alike. Don't even try to understand them. It only gives you a headache.'

Carefully carrying the concoction, Katarin made her way up the stairs and knocked on the door of the spare room, from where came a mumble that she assumed meant 'Come in.' She opened the door slowly, finding the room in dim light, the bed rumpled and clothes strewn across the floor. Hugo lay on his stomach, his face half-buried in the pillow, his naked shoulders brown against white linen.

Weakened by a flood of relief and tenderness, she paused a moment, bending to pick up the crumpled blue cloak and lay it across a chair. When Hugo didn't stir, she sighed and stepped carefully round the rest of his discarded clothing.

'Hugo?'

The sound of her voice made him jerk upright, only to clutch his head and groan, '*Lieber Gott!*'

'Honestly!' Katarin chided. 'Who was it who was going to bring sobriety to the

Weinfest? Here, I've brought you something that might help.'

He blinked at the contents of the glass as though the half-light hurt his eyes. 'What is it?'

'I'm not sure. It's something *Opa* mixed and I expect it tastes as poisonous as it looks, but get it down you.'

He took the glass, tossed the mixture down, shuddered and grimaced, 'Ugh!'

'You'll live,' she said dryly, but as he rubbed his face with his hand she looked at him lovingly. His skin gleamed faintly in the light, and behind his shoulder there was a scar, long-healed, which appeared to have once been an ugly wound.

Unable to prevent herself she reached out and touched the place, feeling the uneven surface of scarred tissue. 'Where did you get that?'

'A long time ago.' He lifted his face, squinting at her through a tangle of dark hair. 'Katarin, go away. I'm ashamed of myself.'

'So you should be,' she retorted. 'Is it true that you were drinking with Berd?'

'Among others,' he said with a shrug and caught her hand, kissing it so that she felt the roughness of stubble on his upper lip before he pressed her hand to his naked

238

chest, pleading with her. '*Liebling*, angel, please go away. Let me get washed and dressed. Then we'll talk.'

'Very well.' Reluctantly she withdrew. 'You look terrible. If your mother could see you . . . Did she give you my message? I phoned.'

'Yes, she told me. Katarin, if you don't go away, I'm going to get out of bed and throw you out. Without any clothes on.'

Since he looked capable of carrying out this threat, she thought it politic to obey him, though she couldn't resist saying pertly, 'Yes, *Herr Baron*.' She ducked out of the room the second before a hurled pillow hit the door.

In the kitchen Frau Grainau was busy peeling oranges and grapefruit, which she put in a bowl and laced with honey, saying that it was a remedy her husband had found effective after a heavy night in the *Bierkeller*.

Eventually Hugo appeared, showered, shaved, and dressed in shirt and slacks. Apart from a suspicion of shadows under his eyes he looked much the same as usual, though the smile he gave Katarin was more a grimace of self-disgust. He sat down opposite her at the table, politely accepting Frau Grainau's fruit and honey 'remedy,' while Katarin poured coffee.

With obvious reluctance the housekeeper

departed to chores elsewhere in the house, thoughtfully closing the door behind her so that Katarin and Hugo were alone in the big kitchen with sunlight streaming through the window onto the tiled floor.

'David went home yesterday,' she said, watching her coffee swirl as she stirred in a touch of cream.

'I know,' Hugo replied.

She glanced up, surprised. 'How did you know?'

'Your grandfather told me.'

'Oh, really!' She sat back, irritated. 'Isn't it about time you stopped using *Opa* as a go-between? Couldn't you have phoned? Couldn't you have waited? I went back to the riverside. They all thought I was deranged.'

'I know that, too. I heard about it last night. I was . . . angry, hurt, unsure of myself. I'm not accustomed to feeling that way, Katarin. I thought I'd repay you by keeping *you* in suspense for a change. So I drank too much, because I was depressed.'

'But you knew I'd tried to get in touch!'

'I didn't know why, though. It might have been to say that you had made up with your *Englischer*!'

'I wish you wouldn't call him that,' she objected. 'It sounds like an insult.'

'It's intended to be! It took all my

240

willpower not to throw him in the river. I wanted to kill him!' His fist slammed down on the table, making the crockery jump and himself wince, briefly pressing his fingers to his forehead; then he leaned fiercely toward her, grasping her wrist in hard fingers. 'Is he gone for good?'

'Yes,' she said, and was relieved to see the tautness drain from his face. 'He's going to marry Carol.'

'Carol?'

'My friend. You met her that day in the wine museum.'

'Oh — the giddy one? I don't remember much about her. All I recall is you being insolent to me.'

An unsteady smile trembled on her lips as his eyes warmed and he drew her hand closer, holding it between both of his own.

'That seems a long time ago, *Liebling*,' he said softly. 'You hurt my pride, that's all. Since then you've done much worse things to me. I don't sleep for thinking about you, and when I do sleep you're there in my dreams, always just out of reach. Is that the way it must be?'

Very gently, sadly, she disengaged her hand from his, her heart wrenching as she saw his expression of disbelief. 'I'm sorry, Hugo' was all she could manage to say.

241

'Sorry?' he said hoarsely. His chair scraped as he pushed it back and stood up, his face so ravaged that she buried her head in her hands, unable to watch him. 'But if it's not the Englishman, then . . . Why, Katarin? Why? Don't you care about me?'

'You know I do!' Distressed beyond bearing, she tore herself from her seat and stood with her back to him, her shoulders heaving with sobs. She felt his hands on her, turning her into his arms, where he held her tightly, his face pressed to her hair.

'Darling, why?' he said again. 'Tell me why.'

She flung her arms round him, holding him with all her strength as her tears soaked into his shirt.

'I love you,' she choked. 'Oh, Hugo, I love you so much.'

Lifting her head, she surged up to fasten her mouth on his, her fingers caught in his hair as she held him to her and felt him respond with a swift passion that made her pulses leap. Her body molded to his, held there by the fierce pressure of his arms. She felt as though she could never have enough of him.

It was Hugo who broke free. Gasping for breath, he drew her head to his shoulder and bent over her, cradling her possessively.

Beneath her ear she heard the erratic thud of his heart.

'Don't do this to me, Katti,' he said raggedly. 'If you love me, then marry me. Don't keep torturing me.'

'I don't mean to.' She was weeping. 'The last thing I want to do is hurt you. But I can't marry you. There's the Maierstufe, and *Opa*, and Berd, and your mother, and . . . everything!'

'There's nothing, Katti. Nothing can come between us.' He led her to the low couch in the window nook where he sat down with his arms around her, presenting her with a clean handkerchief to dry her face.

'Now, *Liebling*, tell me calmly what's troubling you. Is it your hopes for a career? You must know I wouldn't keep you from it if that's what you want. I'd hate it if you were bored like Franziska. If you like, I'll take steps to have the Wine-Growers Association elect their first lady member. I imagine they won't object to having the Baronin Katarin von Drachensberg on their list.'

'Oh, Hugo!' She managed, torn between kissing him and shaking him. 'Thank you but . . . That's only part of it.'

She began calmly enough, though as her fears poured out more tears welled until his handkerchief was soaked. She told him how

243

afraid she was that people would blame her grandfather for allowing the Maierstufe to fall into von Drachensberg hands; how they would say that Hugo must have plotted for just such an eventuality; and how his mother would be appalled by the suggestion of marriage. She did not tell him the baroness had warned her off. She had promised never to mention it.

'These are fearsome obstacles,' Hugo said gravely, though something in his voice made her look at him and see the tiny hint of amusement that lurked at the back of his eyes.

'Yes, they are,' she replied. 'It's not funny, Hugo.'

'Am I laughing?'

'No, but . . . You think I'm making mountains out of molehills, don't you?'

'I think,' he said, a finger caressing her cheek, 'that you are very sweet and very caring. But one thing you can forget — we'll have no trouble from Berd Langren. Last night he and I had a long talk. Neither of us was entirely sober, it's true, and there was a moment when we almost came to blows, but in the end we reached an understanding.'

'You mean about . . . whatever it was that happened when you were boys?'

For a moment he watched her, searching

her face as if he would memorize every line and curve. 'That scar on my shoulder. It was from a gunshot wound. Berd shot me — accidentally.'

'Shot you?' she said in horror.

'I'd been given a new gun for my seventeenth birthday and I suppose I was showing it off to Berd, up on the mountain. I let him try it, but it was a little heavy for him . . . ' He shrugged. 'Well, it was an accident. But he ran off in a panic and left his own air rifle behind. When they found me my father was very angry. He came down to Gundelheim to see the Langrens and I gather there was a terrible argument. My father refused to return the air rifle. Later they made Berd come to see me in hospital and apologize, and he hated that. He hated me because he felt guilty, and because my father confiscated his gun. I don't say he loves me now, but at least we've talked it out.'

'If he remembers,' she said dubiously.

'I'll remind him.' This time the laughter showed clearly in his eyes as his mouth twitched. 'And, anyway, he told me one or two secrets of his own last night, which he won't want revealed. I think we're all square, Herr Bernhard Langren and I.'

'I'm glad,' Katarin said. 'But he was the

least of our problems. You do see, don't you, that — '

He stopped the words by the simple expedient of kissing her. 'I see that you love me,' he murmured in her ear, pressing her back against the couch as he leaned over her. 'That's all I want to know.'

Giving in to her need of him, she looped her arms round his neck and returned his kisses, drowning her fears in the glory of love acknowledged.

She was startled out of her euphoria by the sound of the door opening and Frau Grainau's embarrassed 'Oh! Excuse me, I . . . '

Without haste, Hugo released Katarin and stood up, saying, 'Dear Frau Grainau. You saw nothing, yes?'

The housekeeper seemed mesmerized as she stared at him. 'I . . . I'm very short-sighted, *Herr Baron.*'

'Thank you.' Smiling, he took Katarin's hand and brought her to her feet. 'I must go. You rest. We still have the ball to attend tonight. Ah, Frau Grainau, I believe I left a jacket here somewhere.'

'I'll get it for you,' she muttered as she scuttled out.

'And as for you,' Hugo said, taking Katarin in his arms, 'don't worry. Leave it to me. I'll see what can be done.'

'You'd have to be a magician,' she said sadly.

'Maybe I am.' Softly he kissed her eyes and then her mouth, by which time the housekeeper had returned and stood popeyed with his jacket in her hand. 'Thank you so much, Frau Grainau. Now I suppose I must try to remember where I left my car. Still, the air will do me good. I'll see you later, Katarin.' He smiled down at her, then glanced at the housekeeper with a questioning lift of eyebrows.

'I'm blind,' she vowed. 'And dumb.'

★ ★ ★

All day Katarin was torn between wild hope and numbing despair. What could Hugo do to alter the attitude of a whole town, not to mention the prejudice of his mother? Not even he could work miracles. The future stretched before her, a wilderness without him. Whatever happened, she would never be able to forget him.

However, there was still the final event of the *Weinfest* to be held, and she promised herself that for this one night she would put aside her gloom, forget the future. Perhaps, in time, attitudes might change. Perhaps some miracle would happen.

At last she stood before the mirror in full finery, her hair pinned up in a softly elegant style to complement the vine-leaf crown. The Wine Queen's gown fitted her perfectly, made for her alone without thought for future Queens. It was based on a medieval style with long, tight sleeves, closely fitting at waist and bodice, with gold laces decorating a low neckline. The full skirt swept to the ground in layer after layer of fine chiffon.

When her grandfather called her, saying that Hugo was waiting, she checked her makeup one last time, gave her hair a final pat, and with the wine-red cloak over one arm swept down the stairs to make a grand entrance. The sight of Hugo, looking like some fairy-tale prince, made her pause in the doorway.

His shirt was white silk, with full sleeves frilled at the wrist, the neck loosely laced against his tanned throat. With it he wore close-fitting breeches of a blue that matched his cloak and knee boots polished to a mirror sheen. A wide leather belt spanned his waist, and over it he wore a sword in a scabbard — a real sword, from the looks of it, probably borrowed from one of the suits of armor at the castle. No Prince Charming had ever looked so dashing, or so utterly male.

Her grandfather, too, was resplendent in dinner jacket and black bow tie as, looking from one to the other of them, he laughed aloud. 'A matched pair, if ever I saw one! I can't wait to see their faces. Excuse me, *Liebchen*, I must get to the Town Hall.' He kissed her cheek, twinkled at her, and left the room.

'You look marvelous,' Hugo told her, his glance running covetously over her.

'So do you,' she replied.

'But tomorrow we'll be back to normal. No more Wine King. No more Wine Queen. Just you and me. Will you still love me?'

'I'll always love you,' she breathed through a throat that was suddenly thick with tears.

'No!' With a frown he stepped swiftly toward her and caught her face between his hands. 'No more tears. Not tonight. Be happy tonight. Yes?'

'Yes.' She found a smile for him and saw an answering gleam in his eyes as he bent to kiss her. He seemed to be enjoying himself, and so could she, if she tried.

'I've brought something for you to wear,' he told her, moving away to where a jewelry box lay on the table, a large oblong affair, its cover faded with age. As he opened it Katarin caught her breath at the glitter of gold and rubies. It was a necklace formed like sunrays, studded with gleaming red gems. Hugo gently lifted it from its case, glancing at her with that habitual lift of eyebrow.

'A personal touch,' he said. 'I have the sword. You'll wear this necklace. Turn round and let me put it on.'

Her fingers explored the chased gold and the square-cut rubies as he laid the heavy necklace round her throat, fastened it, and led her to the mirror. There she stared in fascination at the beautiful creation adorning the low neckline of the gown, its glitter a perfect foil against her lightly tanned flesh and the whiteness of the gown.

'My Queen,' Hugo breathed in her ear, brushing his lips down her throat. 'Put on your cloak and let me show you to the town.'

★ ★ ★

Gundelheim was more crowded than ever that night. The market square was a whirl of activity with people thronging across the roads, slowing the traffic that delivered a steady stream of citizens clad in evening dress to the ballroom on the ground floor of the Town Hall. The Mercedes nosed through the crush, making for the old town walls, where, by the tower that housed the wine museum, a carriage and pair would be waiting to convey the King and Queen to the ball.

The 'maidens' were already gathered, with Hans Leitner and a group of parents, friends, and organizers, and the arrival of Hugo and Katarin caused something of a stir as people saw the grand ball costumes for the first time. But Katarin soon became conscious of something amiss: there was no sign of the carriage.

'It's a disaster, *Herr Baron*!' one of the organizers cried. 'A wheel came off when they tried to move it from its shed. No one knows how it happened. It was checked only a few days ago. We've been wracking our brains for some other suitable conveyance. Perhaps the oxcart. What do you think?'

Unconcerned, Hugo suggested that he and Katarin might ride on the Knight's horse, if Hans didn't object. Hans was only too pleased to hand over his mount, and everyone agreed that it was a wonderful idea.

Lifting Katarin by the waist, Hugo set her on the front of the saddle and stepped up behind her with a theatrical swirl of his cloak, gathering the reins in one hand while his other arm held her securely against him. To the cheers of the crowd they set off behind the blaring band toward the center of town, the maidens dancing beside them, the Knight of the Vine playing buffoon behind.

Under cover of the noise, Katarin said suspiciously, 'Did you know the carriage wouldn't be here?'

'How could I know that?' Hugo asked with a laugh.

'I'm not sure. But you did know, didn't you?'

'Ah . . . yes, I have to admit it. I told you that Berd let slip some secrets. One of them was that he'd tried a little sabotage, to spoil our last night of glory. But I shan't tell on him if you don't. Don't worry, I'll pay for the repairs to the carriage. No one need ever know. This is much better, anyway, don't you think?'

As his arm pressed her intimately close to him, she had to agree. Although she was not exactly comfortable, nothing could take away the pleasure of being held in Hugo's arms for all the world to see, even though the spectators would think it was all part of the pretense of a bride and groom off to their wedding feast.

Ahead of them the crowd in the square parted to allow them through, waving and cheering as if they really were royalty. Someone tossed a handful of petals, and a male voice shouted a bawdy comment that made Katarin blush and Hugo laugh.

At last they came to the front of the Town Hall, where the great doors stood open to disclose the entranceway beyond, where the civic party waited. Among them Katarin glimpsed her grandfather's mustache bristling with pride as he grinned broadly at her.

Hans Leitner helped her down and bowed low as she shook out her skirt and cloak, stretching stiff legs. Then Hugo was beside her, offering his hand to lead her up the steps to greet the *Bürgermeister* and the councillors, whose wives were decked in silks and satins, glittering with jewels.

To Katarin's dismay, she realized the baroness was among the party. She wore an elegant black gown with diamonds at her throat, and inevitably, moving along the line shaking hands, Katarin came face to face with her.

The baroness's smile didn't waver. She murmured, 'My dear, how lovely you look,' and held up her cheek to be kissed. Bemused, Katarin leaned and touched her own cheek to that of Hugo's mother, feeling her hand clasped warmly at the same time. There was no chance to stop and wonder about it since other people were waiting to greet her.

At length the whole company moved

toward the ballroom.

'Your cloak,' Hugo murmured. 'Take off your cloak.'

The cord slid undone and the heavy velvet slipped away. Hugo took it and handed it to someone nearby, looked at her with a smile lighting his face, and conducted her with a flourish into the glittering expanse of a room lit by chandeliers, where all the guests stood by their tables watching.

A murmur of appreciation went round as the tall and handsome Wine King, one hand on his sword hilt, with his cloak flowing behind him, led his blushing 'bride' across the shining dance floor to the head table. Spontaneous applause burst out and Katarin was conscious of excited whispers running round the room. The applause grew even louder and one or two people exclaimed incomprehensibly.

The situation was unnerving enough without that puzzling undercurrent, but Katarin could find no explanation for it. Her costume, and Hugo's were splendid, especially with the additions of the sword and the necklace, but surely not enough to cause that extra surge of excitement.

She found herself seated between Hugo and Herr Raichle, who wore his chain of office over his dinner jacket. They exchanged

254

polite small talk as waiters began to serve the meal, and Herr Raichle, in his usual effusive manner, declared that the *Weinfest* had been the most successful and enjoyable in his experience. All thanks to the *Herr Baron*, naturally, without whose generosity in providing the costumes, the haunch of venison, not to mention his taking such an active part in the proceedings, for which the town could never thank him enough . . . And so on. The *Bürgermeister*, in full flood, was hypnotic.

Speeches and toasts interspersed the meal, while an orchestra played soft background music. But eventually the moment arrived for the Wine King to lead his Queen out onto the dance floor. Katarin was glad to note that he left his sword behind, for her legs were weak enough with nerves without the added danger of tripping over a sword. In full view of the luminaries of Gundelheim, he took her in his arms and swept her into a waltz, gazing passionately into her eyes.

'Please don't look at me like that,' she pleaded. 'Everyone's watching.'

'I know,' he said, his arm tightening about her waist. 'That's how I want it. I want the world to know I love you.'

Pink-cheeked, she tore her glance away

and watched the room swirl beyond his shoulder, smiling faces, curious eyes, people discussing the couple on the floor. They moved in a world of their own, her skirts sweeping romantically as she followed Hugo's confident steps, though she wished someone else would get up and dance. For at least half the tune she and Hugo danced alone on the floor, like the Prince and Cinderella, and all the time she was aware that midnight must strike and the dream be over.

'Incidentally,' he said as more couples joined the waltz and she was able to relax a little, 'my mother's only too delighted that I've found someone who can make me happy. We have her blessing.'

'We have?' She drew back to look at him in disbelief.

'You saw the way she greeted you. You don't know her very well, Katarin. It's time you got acquainted. I want the two most important women in my life to be good friends.'

The music ended, the dancers drifted back to their seats. Someone caught Katarin's arm and she glanced round to find Annchen Griebel, who might have been Wine Queen, beaming at her.

'I'm so happy for you, Katarin,' she said shyly. 'And you, too, *Herr Baron*.

Congratulations.' With which she darted away.

Katarin sent a questioning look at Hugo, who shrugged. 'Don't look at me. I never did understand women.'

The evening progressed. Katarin danced with the mayor, with others of the councillors, and with Hugo again, while his mother smiled benignly. Hugo led her back to speak to the baroness, who told her again that she looked lovely.

'And the necklace suits you, my dear. I've never seen it look so charming. I was so pleased when Hugo told me . . . ' A little frown creased her brow. 'Perhaps you find that hard to believe, but it's true. All I want is for my son to be happy, and since he loves you then I'm only too pleased to welcome you into the family.'

She kissed Katarin's cheek warmly, adding in a low voice, 'And thank you for keeping our little secret.'

'Another obstacle gone, I think,' Hugo said with satisfaction as he led her away. 'Ah, here's your grandfather.'

Herr Maier, beaming, claimed her for the next dance, and as he propelled her round the floor he visibly swelled with pride.

'I can't tell you how happy I am, *Liebchen*,' he declared. 'My granddaughter engaged to the baron. Oh, I knew it was in the wind. I've known for a long time. Since he first came to the house. You didn't fool me, either of you.'

'But, *Opa* . . . ' she protested. 'You mustn't jump to conclusions. We're not engaged.'

'Then why are you wearing that necklace?' he demanded. 'My dear child, as soon as you walked in wearing it, everyone knew. It was as good as an official announcement.'

'The necklace?' she said faintly, fingering the chased gold.

'Why, yes. Yes! Didn't he tell you? That necklace is given to the intended bride of the Baron von Drachensberg. It's quite famous in Gundelheim. Everyone knows about it, I assure you.'

A quiver of indignation ran through her and her eyes became stormy as she sought out Hugo's dark head beyond the crowd.

'I'm very happy for you,' her grandfather said. 'And for me, too. Your happiness is mine, *Liebchen*.'

'But the Maierstufe!' she exclaimed. 'If I marry Hugo — '

His laugh cut her off. 'Yes, he told me you were worried about that. Don't be, Katti. The Maierstufe will still be yours, and your children's. What's more, *my* great-grandchildren will inherit the von Drachensberg lands, too. Think of it! And he's asked me to have overall charge of his vineyards, with help from you. I can't wait to get started. He's intending to join the cooperative, you know, but in time I plan for us to grow a special vintage that will make us famous. We'll look after that in our own cellars. The cooperative can have the run-of-the-mill stuff. But they'll be pleased that I've persuaded the baron to join them.'

Katarin stopped dancing, irritation prickling her scalp. 'You've been planning this together, haven't you?'

'We talked of it, yes. He came up to the Maierstufe today and we shook hands on the agreement. Oh, don't worry. I promise you it will be all right. People may talk, but it will pass. Maier and von Drachensberg together will be a force that no one can oppose.'

Skirting the dance floor, they returned to where Hugo was chatting with Herr Raichle.

'Wonderful news!' the *Bürgermeister* burbled. 'I've only just learned of it. May I wish you every happiness, Fräulein Jameson? I trust you will both do us the honor of gracing many functions in the town in future years. Everyone is so pleased that a local girl has caught the baron's eye.'

'Thank you, Herr Raichle,' she said

demurely. 'Will you excuse me if I borrow the Wine King for a while?'

Taking Hugo's hand, she dragged him into the whirl of dancers, muttering, 'I think I'll strangle you.'

'Why?' he asked in surprise.

'This necklace,' she said flatly. 'You should have told me.'

'I agree. It was very remiss of me. But I thought it would avoid an argument. You do like to argue, Katarin.'

'And you like to play jokes!' she retorted. 'It may have escaped your notice, *Herr Baron*, but I haven't said I'll marry you.'

'But you will,' he said with confidence.

'I may have to, since you've compromised me in front of the entire town!'

As the music ended Hugo took her hand and firmly marched her toward a side door, ignoring the amused glances of the few who saw them go.

'Where are we going?' Katarin gasped. 'Hugo!'

By the door a dinner-jacketed Berd stopped his flirting with two pretty girls to take the carnation from his lapel and present it to Katarin with a bow.

'I won't say the best man won,' he said, 'but I wish you both joy. Your week of glory's over now. Just wait until next year, when I'm Wine King. I'll show you how to do it properly.'

'By which time,' Hugo replied, 'I trust the carriage will be in use again.'

Berd went scarlet to the ears, but Katarin saw no more as Hugo dragged her into a vestibule and thence to a shadowy alley where she was amazed to see his silver Mercedes waiting.

'I had someone drive it over for me.' He answered her unspoken question as he opened the passenger door. 'Get inside, Your Royal Highness. You'll find your cloak there if you're cold.'

'Now, look — ' she began, only to have him kiss her with brief but meaningful violence before he pushed her into the seat, bundled her skirts around her legs, and slammed the door.

Seething, she watched his cloak ripple as he strode round to slide in beside her and start the car with one flick of his wrist. He turned up a side street toward the outskirts of town, and for a while Katarin sat huddled in irritable silence, annoyed by the way he had man-handled her.

'You've really been busy today, haven't you?' she accused eventually. 'Everybody was in on it. Everybody except me. You're too clever for your own good.'

He flashed her a sardonic glance. 'You're beautiful when you're angry.'

'Don't laugh at me! And don't patronize me!'

Slamming on the brakes so suddenly that she almost catapulted into the windshield he turned on her. 'You want to quarrel? Fine, let's quarrel. Let's go back and see who's turned this whole thing into such a mess. Who assumed I was engaged to Franziska without bothering to ask me? Who told me there was another man in her life? Who kept fighting me off when I knew very well she didn't mean it? Who didn't tell me what the real trouble was until she'd nearly managed to turn into a nervous wreck? Who saw problems where there weren't any? Who's scared what people might say?'

She was silent, disconcerted by the catalogue of her mistakes, none of which she could refute. 'I was mainly worried for your sake,' she said. 'And for *Opa*'s.'

'Then stop worrying. Our backs are broad. As for my arranging everything . . . Do you think I was going to risk having you dream up some other complication? I wanted things settled. I wanted to make it impossible for you to refuse me. No more 'We shouldn't,' or 'We can't,' or 'I won't.' We should and we can and you will!'

She cast around for something to throw back at him, and after a moment said, 'You didn't deny being engaged to Franziska.'

'Only because I thought you had your Englishman.'

'But when *Opa* asked if you'd set a wedding date, you said — '

'I remember very well what I said. I would let the lady do that. I said she had many commitments — which you had. Your Englishman, your grandfather, your damned vineyard!'

'Me?' she said faintly. 'You meant me? Even then?'

Leaning closer, he brushed her cheek with the backs of his fingers, saying in a totally different tone, 'Even then, my darling. Even though you acted as if you hated me. I decided you were the one for me that first time you came to the castle. So beautiful with your apricot hair. So defiant! You realize if they'd sent someone else, I would never have agreed to this pantomime? And when you told me you were to be my Wine Queen it seemed like fate. It *was* fate. Why else did the gods send you to my enchanted grotto?'

'I thought they sent *you* to *me*,' she said, laying a hand on his shirt where her fingertips adored the feel of warm muscles beneath silk. 'Oh, Hugo. Darling Hugo . . . ' And for the first time she melted into his arms without any doubts or fears.

'So you'll set the date?' he asked eventually.

'Yes. Soon. Very soon.'

'Where would you like to go for our honeymoon? The West Indies? Paris? New York?'

'The Eimsee Valley.'

Drawing back, he looked down into her face with a surprised smile. 'The hunting lodge. If we're there when the snow comes, we might be trapped there for a week or more.'

'Wouldn't it be lovely?'

'Marvelous,' he agreed, kissed her once more and released her, turning to set the car in motion. 'Do you ski? Oh, I must teach you. You'll love it.'

'I'm sure I would, with you for an instructor. But . . . do you mind telling me where we're going right now? You realize we're heading for the vineyards?'

'Our last duty as Wine King and Queen,' he said with a slow, teasing smile. 'Pagan rites?'

'Hugo!' she chided, and then she leaned on his shoulder and laughed with him as the Mercedes climbed up toward acres of vines, now stripped of their fruit, resting beneath a silver moon, waiting for next year's harvest.

Books by Mary Mackie
Published by The House of Ulverscroft:

NIGHTFLOWER
THE FLOWER AND THE STORM
A LIGHT IN THE VALLEY
A MAN LIKE MATTHEW
COUNTERFEIT LOVE
STILL WEEPS THE WILLOW
A VOICE IN THE FOG
THE WAITING WEB
THE UNQUIET SUMMER
ENIGMA FOR A NURSE
INTO THE TWILIGHT
FALCONER'S WOOD
FLAME IN THE FOREST
GIVE ME NO RUBIES
THE CLOUDED LAND
ROBIN'S SONG
NICOLA'S WINTER
SPRING FEVER
RETURN TO LOVE
SEASON OF MISTS
THE OTHER SIDE OF THE RIVER

Non-Fiction:
COBWEBS AND CREAM TEAS
(A Year in the Life of
a National Trust House)

DRY ROT AND DAFFODILS
(Life in a National Trust House)

Silencing the Opposition